Mick Donnellan is a novelist, playwright and screenwriter. His fiction has won numerous awards and his plays are regularly adapted for the national and international screen. Read more on www.mickdonnellan.com

Other work by Mick Donnellan

Fiction

El Niño

Fisherman's Blues

Mokusatsu

The Naked Flame.

Tales from the Heart (Editor)

Plays

Sunday Morning Coming Down

Shortcut to Hallelujah

Gun Metal Grey

Velvet Revolution

Radio Luxembourg

Nally

Checkpoint Charlie

Screen

Tiger Raid

Nally

Lucky Run

The Dead Soup would not have been possible without the invaluable support of Mayo County Council Arts office and the Arts Council of Ireland.

The Dead Soup

Short stories by
Mick Donnellan

*For Paddy Donnellan,
the greatest storyteller
of them all.*

CONTENTS

THE DEAD SOUP

The Crucified Silence

God is dead. And we have killed him. It was eight o'clock and I was on the shift until four.

Jesus. I was already steamed, volatile.

Whisky usually did that. Made me volatile, impulsive.

Clumsy too.

I went to make a cup of coffee and tripped over the plug of a photocopier and banged my head off an office chair.

It made an awful clatter.

Then the super walked in to see what the racket was.

Saw me attempting to stand up, gave a condescending look and said: You better go home.

Home? says I, half delighted.

Home,he said.And think about your options.

I gave a look that said: *Options*? He read it, went: You can't be on the force and be drinkin like you do.

I said: *Force?* Christ we're not in America.

He loved that, got pure thick, leaned forward, right into my face, all nostrils and rotten gums, said: Do us all a favour and go home, will ya?

Nobody wants to be looking at a useless pisshead like you. And half the town talkin about you as it is....

And that's when I hit him.

Fuck it. Like I said. *Impulsive.*

He fell on the table first and then hit the ground and went sort of purple.

A load of papers and rubbers and pencils fell on of top of him.

And he started kicking his legs like mad.

So I did what any decent Irish man would do at a time like that.

I ran. Straight to the pub.

Down High street. Passed the mound and the bowers walk.

Cold night, like a childhood winter.

Pure Novena weather.

My mind was racing, like a hamster on the purest coke.

Had I gone too far? Absolutely.

Was there any turning back?

Absolutely not. Time to put her in first and sink the shoe.

I could almost taste the Guinness in Arts.

I'd have a whisky while the pint settled.

Double *Powers*, maybe. Oh, they loved me.

A good customer. Useful on a quiet Tuesday night.

I could see the lights on above the pub door, like a lighthouse in a serious storm.

And church bells in the distance for the

evening mass.

There'd be a few there for the anniversary but I couldn't handle it.

Paid my own respects today with a bag of cans and a litre bottle of *Paddy.*

And then I'd gone to work. Not the best plan as it turned out.

Walked on by the river.

Thought about the days when I wanted to be a priest.

Wanted to serve altar wine and communion.

Wanted to serve God.

But I didn't because I was in love too.

And I couldn't be a priest and be in love.

And her name was Karena.

One of the O'Donnell's.

A highly respected family.

And we'd gotten married.

And everything was great for a while.

But now she was gone.

Long gone. Everything, *everybody*, all gone.

And where was God when I needed him most?

And what if the super *died?*

Well, I was drunk your honour.

Besta luck with that.

Up the hill. My feet felt like numb stones.

The police jacket felt too big.

Like it belonged to someone else.

Or I'd shrunk since the first time I wore it.

I probably had. Half the man I used to be. Figure that.

I got in.

The pub was warm and fairly packed. I got a whisky in to me fast.

Talked a bitta shite and went to the jacks.

The jacks smelled like detergent and fairy liquid and childhood Sundays.

My blood started dancing with the *Powers.*

My brain making plans for more.

Counting the money in my pocket. Deducting the taxi home.

To hell with the taxi. I'd get two extra shots and walk.

Was looking ahead to about eight good pints and eight doubles.

And oblivion. It's a great thing on the session.

You don't have to worry about anything really.

Only where your next pint is coming from.

And how long it'll last and if the craic is good.

The craic's always good when you've the price of more, though.

And sure I had nothing to go home to.

I used to. I used to have *plenty*. But not anymore.

I got depressed then, thinking about that, and my mood lost cabin pressure.

I looked at the urinal and thought about

Karena.

And I thought back to that time we got engaged and how she started making plans for the wedding.

And how I took a notion and joined the guards and did my time in Templemore.

It was good craic down there. Lads like myself.

The oul fella was glad. My brother Stephen was glad.

My mother had died.

Karena wanted kids. *We got pregnant.*

That's what they say now these days. *We got pregnant.*

It happened almost straight away. I was happy. She was happy.

We got a house. Her family had money so they paid for it.

And it was here in Arts we went the day after the wedding. Big session, pictures. Future looking bright.

Karena's oul fella going around the place like a bollix because he was paying for it.

He always said I wasn't good enough for her.

Not a pharmacist, or a solicitor, like she deserved.

But the guard thing took the edge of at least.

Although I think he knew I was winging it.

Then the child came. A little girl. *My little girl.* I held her in my arms.

A gift from God. I felt immortal. She was

part of me. And Karena.

Sorta like an *us* all in one. Her big blue eyes looking up at me.

Like they were saying: Mind me, will ya? *Mind* me.

Sure I could hardly mind myself.

We called her Sharona.

Don't ask me why. I just rolled with it.

The nights were long. She cried a lot. We took turns with her.

Then it was ok after a while and me and Karena got some time to lie down. Ya know? Just lie there. Making shapes on the ceiling. Talking about the first things that came into our heads.

*

Christ, that pint should be settled by now.

I zipped up. Ran the water.

There was no soap so I dried my hands on my hair.

Looked old in the mirror. Tired eyes.

A girl once told me she loved my eyes.

They were dark and sensitive, she said.

I lost her too. Maybe she'd have left anyway.

Sure what's it matter now?

I went back out. Shane had the Guinness ready.

I threw a twenty on the counter and took a big slug.

It was glorious. Lovely freedom and escape.

Then my serenity was crushed by this: Do you want to buy a dog? Heh?

It was Micky Murphy.

Four foot clown with a lisp and a square head.

Known around here as:

A character.

A crayture.

Harmless.

And he was always trying to sell dogs and look for news.

No thanks, Micky. You're grand.

Are you sure?

Positive.

Are you still in Dolan's flat, heh?

None of your business where I am.

And I turned my back. Hoping he'd get the message.

Knowing well it was a waste of time.

*

Not too sure why I started with the drink.

Nights on the beat. Bored.

I'd have a naggin of whisky in my flask.

Just to keep the cold out.

To take the edge off.

Fella on duty with me was called John.

He knew the craic but he said nothing.

Knew I needed the job with the new arrival and all that.

He did most of the driving. I slept a lot.

We checked people for tax and broke up fights.

And at night he'd drop me off and I'd get

home and walk up the stairs.

The plush carpet that I couldn't have bought.

The paintings on the wall that I didn't chose.

Them flowers on the table - the likes of which were never seen in my house at home.

All that stuff that Karena's family brought. I was like a guest, ya know?

But Karena was happy so it didn't really matter after a while.

Just nights like that. When you come home.

The place that's supposed to be home. And it's not really.

You're just *crashing*. With your wife and kid.

Crashing forever.

But some nights after work I'd cook a few chips.

I'd always be hungry after a shift.

And I didn't want to be one of them guards that's always in the chipper or the Chinese.

But Karena didn't like deep fat fryers so I'd fill up a pot with oil and load the frozen chips in.

I liked it better that way anyway. And it reminded me of being a kid.

This is the way my mother used to always cook them when we were young.

Before she went for a routine check-up and everything changed.

I don't think I've ever been right since that.

But the smell and sizzle always made me

nostalgic and somehow safe and let me make the place my own for a little while.

Bit like my mother was with me, chatting.

And they tasted lovely. Salt, vinegar, ketchup.

The real deal.

And after, I'd say: Goodnight, mam, love ya. And I'd take my flask and throw back a long swig and head on up to bed.

Or maybe an odd night I'd ate a feed and fall asleep at the kitchen table, but most nights I'd make it up the stairs.

On the way by Sharona's room I'd look in. The cot. The toys. The innocence. Her little chest going up and down and her eyes closed.

And she looked like my mother ya know? And I'd rub my hand along her cheek and look outside into the night and the nowhere and the stars and the quiet breeze and the odd lonely eejit wandering past.

And I'd think of all the things Sharona had to go through in this cruel world.

And there was nothing we could do about it.

And she'd stir a little bit then. Like my mind was connected to hers and she was waking up so I'd slip away, and into Karena, and into the bed that came from somewhere I'd never heard of.

And it had all these fancy things in it.

Like memory foam.

And I'd lie beside her. And put my hand around her. And she'd back into me cos she'd know I was home. And I'd take in the smell of her hair, like strawberries and discos, and I'd lie there blinking. Ya know? Just lie there. Blinking.

*

Here's Micky again, over after me, like a fart in a church.

Will you sort out a speeding fine for me? Heh?

You don't drive, Micky.

It's for my brother, heh? He's an awful messer.

I can't, it's against regulations.

(So is hitting the super but I didn't mention that.)

Ah go on, said Micky, I'll buy you a pint. Heh?

Make it a Guinness, so.

He ordered it, came back and said: I seen the O'Donnell's going into the chapel, heh? Is it a year now since?

I don't want to talk about it.

Someone said the place was all done up again?

That's enough now, Micky.

Sure nobody could ever live there after that? Heh?

Go somewhere else now, Micky, good man.

And the poor kiddeen, what age was she, two? Three? Heh?

Here, John Kelly is up the top bar there, ask him does he want any dogs and leave me alone.

They musta been damn nice chips, heh?

For the last time, Micky.

Are you not ashamed of yourself? Heh?

I was about to go for him when the sirens flew past.

Flying down the hill. On the way to the station.

It distracted everyone. Even Micky. He ran straight for the door to see.

I went back to my pint, took a long swill.

It went down my throat like warm honey, but the good was gone out of it.

Suddenly the pub lights were burning against my head like big two bar heaters. And I felt like I was on a stage. That feeling of crucified silence.

Same as an actor that can't remember his lines.

The crowd watching, staring.

I took another belt of stout.

And there was people talking around me.

Joe, they were saying, there's an ambulance outside the cop station.

You could see it from the door of Arts, like.

Really, I said, wonder why's that?

Pint, Shane, when ya get a chance.

Are ya not going up? He went.

And it wasn't a question.

Worse still, there was a loada people asking me questions now.

Looking for answers about what was going on.

Faces that said: Aren't you the guards?

I turned to Shane and said: I suppose I better go up so and see.

And I finished my pint and walked out. Into the night again, evicted from the sanctuary.

I could see the red and blue and lights dancing in the distance.

The super must have hit the panic button, the *send bloody everyone* alarm.

It reminded me of this night a year ago. Drunk then, drunk now.

The firefighters, the guards, the bystanders. Karena's father going around like a madman, shouting and roaring. And how he went for me, pure rage, like he wanted to kill me. But it even didn't matter. Sure I was already dead, and I'm dead since, my heart in the morgue, my mind gone to the greatest Hell.

Ballymahon

Parked up in a town called Ballymahon. A place often said to be awful quare. Found a Spar. Got a fast roll and a silky coffee. Started walking back, through a wide street with charity shops and signs for Longford and Cavan. Tractors roared by, populated with young lads on phones and big grumpy trailers full of round bales. There was a smell like hay mixed with motor oil and the sky had a grey hue that fell over the whole place like a blanket. Bit like it was supposed to rain, but someone had hit the pause button and forgot about it and now it's a humid sense of endless expectation for a moment that never arrives.

Next thing a fella sticks his head out a window and goes: 'Hey!'

I turned around. It was a grey house with white framed windows. A red Toyota Starlet outside with no wheels, just rims and rust.

I walked back, said: 'Yeah?'

He was overweight. Talking down from upstairs.

'Were you lookin for me?' He goes.

He was in a beige vest, stubble, early fifties

maybe. Faded tattoos on flabby arms.

'No.'

He frowned, like I'd insulted his intelligence, went: 'Were you lookin for my wife?'

'Eh…no.'

'Why are you here?'

'Where?'

'Outside my house.'

'You called me back. Do you want somethin?'

'Don't talk to me like that, buddy.'

'Like what, man? I don't even who you are.'

'Do you think you're smart?'

'What the fuck are you even talking about?'

He pulled a face like he wanted to hit me but the thought of the trip down was putting him off. So he pointed and said: 'Me and you are goin to have a serious problem.'

'I don't have any problem at all. I was minding my own business and you called me back. What do you want?'

'Sure I don't want anythin.'

'Why'd you call me back so?

'I told you buddy, don't be talkin to me like that. Don't get fuckin smart.'

'Right so, I'll go.'

'Do. Fuck off.' He said.

In the spirit of de-escalation, I replied 'YOU fuck off.'

His eyes went wide. 'I'm warning ya, pal. I'll come down there and box your head.'

'For what?'

'For annoyin me.'

'Have you nothin better for doin?'

'How do you mean by that?'

'Like stickin your head out the window and attackin people for nathin.'

'What?' He goes. 'Do you have a job or somethin?'

'I do.'

'Oh, so you think you're fuckin better than everyone else?'

'No, but I've better things for doin than this.'

'Then piss off and do them.'

'I am. I was. You're holdin me up.'

'Oh the big man....thinks he's fuckin great cos he has a job. Well do you know what you can do with your job now?'

'I've a feelin you're goin to tell me.'

'You can shove your FUCKIN job up your hole.'

'Thanks. I'll go now so.'

'Do. While you're still able.'

'Maybe you should try workin yourself. It'll help pass the time.'

This sent him over the edge and he disappeared inside. There was a thumping sort of rumping inside. Like he was banging into things and knocking them over. Presses, cabinets, things with glass in them. And then there was noise on the stairs, like an elephant playing the bongo.

He was shouting variations of threats like:

Stay there ya bollocks!

I'm fuckin comin!

You're fucked now, buddy!

The car was across the road. I was nearly there by the time he was down but I could still hear him shouting from the door. 'You're nathin but a FUCKIN PRICK! Get the fuck outta my life you cunt! I'll come over there and bursht your fuckin head!'

I got in, turned the key, thanking fuck it started. Threw the roll on the passenger seat and pulled out. Gave him a wave as I drove away and went home.

Christ above.

Awful quare entirely.

The Lost Ones

Walked into Java's and lit another cigarette. The place smelled like burnt cheese and sweet broken laws. I dragged hard, pain in my windpipe, like cancerous patriotism. Adam was in the corner, looking nervous. He was normally calm, in control, but now he was like a man trying to stomach bad news.

I sat down, wood chairs, checkered tablecloth, said. 'How come you're not smokin?'

'TOBIES.'

TOBIES. *Tobacco Ban Apocalyptic Cult Soldiers.* The cruel enemy of all things nicotine, champions of a healthy dystopia.

I said: 'What about them?'

'We have an infiltrator.'

I smoked more, glorious pain in my right lung, said: 'Not possible. We haven't had any new recruits for at least a year.'

'Facts are facts. The TOBIES know things they can't know without someone tellin them.'

I gave a suspicious look around. Java's was a good spot. My crew always assembled here. You were safe and you could smoke. It was our side of town. No TOBIES. Just loyal soldiers, smoking, dedicated to the cause, no weak links. But Adam was unsure, and I didn't like it. I exhaled some chemicals, good honest passive disease, and asked: 'There a gathering tonight?'

'Yeah. There's talk of the big man coming down.'

'Who? *Jones*?'

'Yeah.'

This caused a reflex inside me. Something between excitement and tantalizing fear.

'Jesus.'

'I know.' Said Adam. '*Our* Jesus.'

'How's your quota?'

'15. Need 5 more to reach the minimum.'

'So get smokin, boss. Could be a long night.'

Later, at the gathering, the room was small and personal, just enough space for about twenty people. Everybody was pumped, hostile, looking for a TOBIE to tear apart. We knew Jones would have a plan, a strategy, maybe a new form of guerrilla tactics. He was not only an expert interrogator but renowned for hacking the health service, blowing up the COPD centres; and was even said to be building a concertation camp for cancer doctors. If we had a leak in our regiment, we knew he would find it through pure truth and commitment to our goal.

He walked in and everybody stood to attention. All eyes watching him. His charisma thick in the air.

'At ease.'

We sat down. He was black, dressed in army fatigues. The light shining off his bald head.

'This is division 147 of the Galway East Battalion, led by Adam Trevelyan. Is that correct?'

Adam stood up. 'Sir! Yes Sir!'

'And you have filed a report to headquarters; stating you have an informer in your ranks?'

'That is correct, sir.'

'And you have a suspect?'

'No, sir.'

'Do you trust all the men in this room, Trevelyan?'

'Yes sir, with my life, sir.'

'Would you say you have taught them well?'

'Excellent, sir. To the best of my abilities, sir.'

'Very well. Be seated.'

He pressed the transmitter on his radio, said: 'Prepare the *Cigarstats*.'

This caused unease. Uber confidence turned to pale fear. The *Cigarstats* test was designed to examine everything you know. I was never assessed before, but I had heard about it. Sadistic but effective, it always filtered out the traitors because it was foolproof. Jones was taking no chances. We were all getting tested – whether we were innocent or not - and somebody in the room was going to die.

I was the fifth to be called. The others had returned shaken, but alive.

I walked into the room. It was totally dark except for a large lamp placed over a dentist chair in the middle. There was a smell of sweat in the air, like the aftermath of a boxing match. A bald man stood behind the chair in a white lab coat. He had the stone cold expression of a patient executioner. Behind him, I could see a silhouette in the darkness tinkering with something. A noise to my right, gave me a fright, and my heart flipped like a scared fish. I looked over and Jones emerged from the shadows and said: 'Take a seat, McGregor.'

I felt guilty for no reason at all. Adrenaline flooded my system, as if from a burst dam, or like waiting for a life-or-death diagnosis from a doctor. The silhouette from the corner walked into the frame and I saw what he had been toying with. It was the standard issue weapon for all new cadets. Small, brutally effective, horribly loud.

'Is it loaded?' Asked Jones.

He nodded in solemn, confident reply. He had cracked lips, jaundiced eyes, brown fingers. He was a soldier like myself. Standard navy uniform. Obedient, loyal, eager to please and to kill. He lit up, Asian Tiger tobacco, an inspiring smell, like burning perspex. I recognized the red box too, probably even played a part in importing them off the coast. That was our only option now since the Tobies closed everything down.

'McGregor,' began Jones, 'we are going to test your loyalty to the cause. Are you familiar with the *Cigarstats* method?'

'Sir, yes, sir.'

'And you know the consequences of getting an answer wrong?'

'Yes, sir. Immediate termination of the soldier with torture and death to his family, sir.'

'Tell me, John, what's the most dishonourable death a *Procigoro* soldier can have?'

'Sir, to die of a cause that is *not* smoking related, sir.'

The man in the white coat taped some stickers to my chest and temples. They were the tags of a polygraph contraption behind my head. His breath smelled of garlic and bad gums as he wheezed while working around me. The wires went into the machine, which was switched on by the gaunt cadet. It whirred and whizzed as it came to life, like an ECG exam. After, he strapped my wrists to the seat with buckskin belts and the soft leather of the chair was firm against my back.

The cadet hung the cigarette on his mouth and rolled something around to the centre of my vision. It was a long steel arm with an artificial hand at the end, similar to a robot in a cyborg film. It squealed as he pushed it, like it needed oil in the hinges at the elbow. He took the gun and slotted it perfectly into the skeletal palm between the spindly metal fingers, placing the index on the trigger. After that, my head was tied back and now there was only six inches between me and the barrel of the pistol.

The whole system was connected to the

polygraph.

The method was obvious. If I told a lie, the machine would activate the trigger, giving me a premature death of shame and dishonour.

'Are we ready?' asked Jones. They nodded. He turned to me. 'State your name and number for the record, please.'

'McGregor, John. Soldier 297 of the *Procigoro*. Second-in-command of Galway East Battalion 147, led by Adam Trevelyan, sir.'

'How long have you been active?'

'Ten years, sir.'

The needle scrawled behind me. I didn't want to get too tense in case the readings registered my brainwaves as lies. All they needed was a hint. The cadet was watching, bug eyed and ready, his interest bordering on the erotic. I tried to close my eyes to avoid the gun but he suddenly smacked me. The pain of the blow gave me such a shock that I barely heard the next question.

'Define *smoking*.'

'Sir, the act of inhaling fumes from a burning substance, sir.'

'What is the current population of the world?'

'It was last recorded at 10 billion in 2026, and is currently rising by 80 million a year, sir.'

'How is passive smoking achieved?'

'Inhaling smoke because of proximity to a smoker, sir.'

It was textbook. The standard answers.

'What are the known *advantages* of passive smoking?

'Still birth, sudden infant death syndrome, a significantly higher rate of contracting smoking related diseases.'

'How high?'

'1.5 percent.'

'What is the current smoking quota for each soldier?'

'Sir, 20 a day, sir.'

'How many times does he inhale tobacco smoke a year?'

'On average, 70,000, sir.'

'How many poisonous chemicals in a cigarette?'

'4,000, sir.'

'How many carcinogenic?'

'53, that we know of, sir.'

'How many times does a soldier expose himself and others to carcinogenic chemicals in one smoking year?'

My mind went blank. The machine whirred louder, and I couldn't concentrate. Instead of rhyming off the answer I was trying to work it out. There was a venomous sense of anticipation all around me.

I got it just in time.

'Three hundred and eighty six thousand and nine hundred, sir.'

'*Close*, McGregor, that's a big stat.'

'Sir, sorry sir.'

'Forget sorry, what about the air?'

'Sir, as the population increases, there is less air to breathe.'

'And?'

'It is the aim of the *Procigoro* to keep the population down.'

'How?'

'Smoking, active and passive.'

'Are you a *TOBIE*?'

'Sir, no, sir!'

He waited to look at the reading. It remained calm and he lit a cigarette. The gun stared at me patiently. My wrists itched in the leather strap and my eyes watered.

'Organs of smoking related disease?'

'Sir, lungs, larynx, pancreas, cervix, kidney, bladder, artery...'

'Diseases?'

'Bronchitis, emphysema, heart disease, cancer...'

'The most common cancer?'

'Lung, sir.'

'Stat?'

'Over 90% of all cases are smoking related.'

He stopped, stubbed out his cigarette and immediately lit another one.

'That sounds rehearsed, McGregor, almost like you don't believe it. I need to know you're the real deal.'

'Sir, there is nothing I don't know about the *Procigoro*, sir.'

'We'll see, tell me the philosophy, why are you here? Any fool can learn stats.'

'I am committed to saving the world through smoking. I believe that by smoking cigarettes, I contribute to a lower population and save the planet from a holocaust, sir. I hate the propaganda of the TOBIES. They claim that we should all live longer. But if we do, the world will become uninhabitable. A scramble for food, space and air will ensue and eventually lead to a worldwide war for resources. I detest the lies that tell me smoking is bad. The *Procigoro* believe that at the current rate of growth, the population will be unsustainable in one hundred years. Fifty per cent of the people who smoke are killed by their habit. The more we smoke, sir, the greater the chance for humanity. It is our strongest, most powerful weapon.'

'How?'

Everything went into a fuzz and the heat of the gun twitched on the bridge of my nose. My mind sifted through a hurricane of information. I knew there was an answer. It was why I needed to talk to him. I had a statistic that would be valuable to the cause, something he hadn't thought of and was certain to recruit more troops. I could see it in my mind but couldn't get the words in order. The machine groaned, worked up a whine.

'How? Gimme a stat McGregor.'

My mind went blank. The pen was scraping furiously; the squiggles spelling: Lies! Lies! Kill!

Kill!

'How? Tell me, how!'

The robotic hand clicked to life and put pressure on the trigger. They all backed away in anticipation.

'Sir, I have a new stat, sir!'

'Give it to me!'

Scribble. Scribble. Scribble. The inner workings of the gun's chamber getting ready to fire.

Jones turned his back like he couldn't watch. 'It's over, McGregor.'

Then I remembered. 'Sir, cigarettes contain a highly addictive substance called nicotine. Its traits are comparable to that of cocaine or heroin. They kill more than three million people a year, sir.'

The machine squealed. High pitched and vicious, like a scalded cat.

'Not good enough! Everyone knows that!'

'Sir, that's more than car accidents, alcohol, illegal drugs, murders, suicides and AIDS, *combined*, sir!'

I winced expecting a shot but instead everything lulled. The machine calmed and Jones walked over to check the validity. He lit another cigarette.

'That's good, McGregor, perfect for our new recruitment drive. Where'd you get it?'

'Sir, the archives, sir.'

'The archives?'

'Sir, yes, sir.'

He looked at the other men.

'Let him go and send in Trevelyan. I want to talk about the archives.'

The bald executioner was obedient but the cadet seemed disappointed, like his horse hadn't won. They unhooked the straps and the leather left a raging red mark on my wrists. My head felt incredibly light and my legs were like rubber. They linked me under the arm and led me to the door.

'McGregor,' called Jones.

I turned.

'Sir?'

'I'm increasing your quota to thirty a day, congratulations.'

'Thank you, sir.'

I left and joined the rest of the crew in silence.

*

We call them the lost ones. When the black worm of corruption slithers through a chink in a man's armour of belief. There's no going back and it's only a matter of time before the serpent reveals itself. We heard the shot ten minutes later and knew that Adam was dead. Jones had suspected him for a while but it was the fact about the archives that gave him away. He had to have known. When they went to his house it was all there. He had been withholding information for months; there was even notes on his meetings with the *TOBIES* and a hoard of stashed cigarettes in the basement. He hadn't been smoking or meeting his quota for almost a year.

I took over the regiment and trained some young blood. It makes me proud to see the juvenile recruits coming up. Eager to carry on our work. And our cause gets stronger every day. A new statistic says half the kids in China will die from smoking related diseases. I'm on thirty a day now and I feel good. My health is destroyed and I probably won't live much longer. There's some test results due from the clinic and I'm praying for a fatal disease, but enough time to inflict maximum passive damage.

We rarely see treason anymore and I think it's a positive sign. I live for a cause I believe in and want to die in its name. At my current quota, I inhale 5,753 carcinogenic chemicals a day. I can't think in years because I don't have them. But even if I was granted one more, I know it would involve at least 10,950 cigarettes. Some say Jones is on a 100 a day now, a real martyr, and when the true revolution comes they'll build a statue in his honour. Maybe I'll live long enough to see it. If not, I'll die knowing the world is a better place and I did my duty. Can you say the same?

Tall Tales Of New York

'This reminds me of New York.'

'Why, how?

'Things were bad. Belfast was on fire. We were bringing in Armalite rifles from the states and trying to source RPG's at the same time. We needed them to take down the choppers. We controlled the streets but the air still belonged to the Brits. If we could take down them hawks the English'd be all dead within a week.'

'Probably take more than a week.'

'We had them by the balls except for that. So they sent me to the states.'

'From Belfast?'

'Yeah. We had one of our lads on the boat. Queen Elizabeth two. Size of a small town. He made sure my name wasn't flagged by security and he'd be waiting to help get the stuff onboard for the way back.'

'They're not boats. They're ocean liners.'

'And I'm a freedom fighter, not a sea captain. What's your point?'

'Just tell your damn story.'

'So I got there. And it was all skyscrapers and dead heavy heat coming from the vents on the street and I went to meet the contact. She was half Indian/half Irish. Into all the Gandhi glory. Told me all about him. And she liked the Irish story too. Seducing her was easy.'

'You slept with her?'

'Standard operating procedure.'

'Maybe not *standard*.'

'That's how I got to know her, learned if she could be trusted.'

'And she could?

'Yeah, she held nothing back. The electricity was there. No intermittent power cuts to her passion.'

'What if it was a guy?'

'What do you mean?'

'How would know if you could trust him?'

'Same.'

'You'd sleep with him?'

'If that's what he was into, yeah. I don't discriminate. What are you? Some kind of homophobe?'

'So what happened?'

'The next day she introduced me to a fella called Derek. We were in Manhattan. Roof top apartment. The Twin Towers were even still there. We were drinking Vodka. Scorching sun. Derek was all handshakes and had a messed up accent like he was trying to swallow a pool ball. Asked me did I want Armalites? Said I was good for *them* but I needed RPG'S/Surface to Air Missiles. Anything that could take down a helicopter. He wanted specifics. How would I get them home? Who was I working with? Could I be trusted?'

'I remember Derek. Tall guy, weird teeth.'

'Yeah, mouth like a warzone. But everyone trusted him. He came with golden credentials. He had contacts with the Libyans, Colombians, Basques and Palestinians. This was who we needed. A libertarian with no conscience, a capitalist that didn't care, an international arms dealer with a soft spot for the underdog. But I didn't like him.'

'Why not?'

'Cos one time, in Tyrone, I had a bad feeling about an operation, and I didn't go, and later that night the whole unit got wiped out in an ambush. And now I had the same feeling.'

'So what happened?'

'I told him I'd tell him nothing until I saw what I wanted. He took offence. Told me to go shite in a bucket and left. I was relieved. I was sure he was working for the cops. I rang home. They said to wait. Time passed. Three days. Still hot but the nights were cool. The call came. I was in Christina's apartment.'

'Christina? She's the…?'

'Gandhi freak. Yeah. We were in bed, sweat and skin, cum everywhere, her hair on my chest, me looking at the ceiling letting the algorithms run, the permutations dance, something somewhere was off. She handed me the phone, landline, Bakelite, stringy wire. I said hello into the big round mouthpiece. Derek was in a soundproof room somewhere, no background noise, wanted to know if I could meet. He had what I wanted. There was a place close to Port Authority. It was quiet. He said a time and he hung up. Christina said she knew where it was. So we got ready. Had a shower together, let the hot water sing through our last goodbye. I'd miss her, this, it, those eyes, them nipples, that tongue. We got dressed. Her car was a Porsche. We passed Central Park and Times Square and we stopped at a traffic light and I was looking at some big billboard and then *bang*. Suddenly I know for a fact that Derek's compromised.'

'How?'

'I didn't know why at first. I got a shiver down my back and thought about our conversation three days before. His eyes. The way he drank. No wedding ring. His clothes were new. Unworn. Like a costume or something. For a while I couldn't tell what it was. I kept thinking *clean....he's too clean.* But that wasn't it. He looked at my shoes too much. Talked too loud. Drank like he was used to it, but he wasn't. He was acting but he couldn't act. Everyone said he was ok. Had done deals before. But I knew this was different. I looked back at the billboard and it was some catholic thing about Judas and the power of conscience and then I realised that was it. He was conflicted. He was screwing me over but there was a war going on in his head. He was under pressure to throw me and the whole unit under the Mi6 crucifixion bus. In a way he was trying to warn me. Some part of him knew anyone with experience would pick up the radar of betrayal and if they didn't, well, fuck them.

I told Christina to pull up and she asked why. I told her I needed a bathroom and she pulled in at a pub. I got inside and took a piss and found a back door. Got on to an alleyway with rubbish and cats and whores. Found a wide street and flagged a taxi to the airport and flew back home empty handed.'

'You just *left* her there?'

'Yeah, maybe she was part of it. I wasn't takin any chances.'

'What did they say when you got back?'

'Nothin. It was a sting. Christina tried to go ahead with the deal and got done that night. And they got the guy on the boat too.'

'The ocean liner?'

'That, yeah. They waited until Christina tried to hand over the gear and swooped in.'

'And where's she now?'

'Christina? She got prison,twenty years, but we broke her out and got her back to India.'

'Least you could do.'

'She sent me a postcard last week. Asking me to come visit.'

'Are you goin?'

'I don't know. There's a fella on the Pakistani border with cheap grenades, and the sex would be great, I just don't know about the food. I never liked Indian cuisine that much, you know?'

Stargate Athlone

Danny got out of jail on a Friday. Mad for drink, craic, mayhem. First place he found was a closed restaurant and decided to rob it. Kicked in the door, like he expected a crowd, gasps, respect, but the empty chairs weren't interested, and the dusty tables didn't even budge. He got into the kitchen and raided the presses, cabinets, anywhere that looked like it might have money, or a key to a safe, or even just a box of change to keep him going. Everything felt loud, squealing hinges, grumpy fridge doors, clattering buckets thrown out of the way. And all he found was two bottles of wine and a few buckets of margarine. He took the wine, and pissed into the margarine, and broke back out through the window.

There, on the street, surrounded by broken glass and deathly silence, he took a long slug of the wine, wasn't impressed, felt it was warm and soupy. He finished it off, both bottles, down the hatch, and smashed the empties on the ground like a man that knew how. Up the hill he went, a real yahoo, where to next? He lit a cigarette, as taught by cinematic gangsters, then kicked a black bin and decided he needed a car. It's uncertain how he got in to the securely locked carpark. Instinct maybe, fluke, or he followed some innocent tenant through the gates. Either way, he found himself surrounded by vehicular options. Things were looking up, but the wine was kicking in, and he wasn't in a fit state to discriminate between different models and makes. There was fancy new SUV's, BMWs, and one or two electric yokes. After that, it was all downhill. 10 years old and better. There was even a Corolla covered in dust and cobwebs that stirred envy and nostalgia in anyone born before 1993. It was the older cars he went after. No alarms, simpler to rob as he'd been in jail when the newer ones were invented. He hit a Fiesta first. Got €2 worth of change. Then went for the Peugeot. There wasn't much in that, maybe a jacket and a pair of shoes and an old bottle of water. He took the jacket and kicked off the wingmirror in disgust and kept going. Eventually he found a Polo and somehow got it started. Maybe he figured it was time to go at that stage. Cameras, noise, broken glass, curious passers-by, all the usual mood killers. The Polo was small with great power, which was good because he didn't know how the gates worked. If he chose the exit gate it would open automatically but, if he chose the entry gate, he would have to drive right through it. The irony of diverging roads in the mechanical woods was lost as he chose the wrong gate and smashed into it with a loud clang and clatter that oddly woke nobody. The gate itself looked wounded, knocked, twisted like it was trying to do yoga and got stuck in the violated street. So, he drove into it again, and again, and again until he woke most of the town and the hinges surrendered and he was able to speed off in the front wrecked Polo towards the wine drunk fuzz of the future.

Guards by now had been notified, made alert, told what was happening. Later the lead investigator would claim the phones "...lit up like a Christmas tree..." The people that owned the restaurant had called first. The law listened intently to horror stories of stolen wine and desecrated margarine. And now there was this *Fast and the Furious* effort going on in the nearby carpark. Stab vests and walkie talkies were procured. Police vehicles dispatched with sirens. This was a manhunt now. All go. First they found the car on fire about a mile up the road. Fire brigades were *looped in* as the operation escalated in scale. Another report now of a kicked cat in a nearby council estate. This could be a lead. More blue lights screamed through the patient night as the sky and stars enjoyed the scene. They found him there, at an old girlfriend's house. She wouldn't let him in because the last time he dropped drugs on the floor and the child nearly swallowed an ecstasy tablet. And it might affect her single mother's payments if people saw him around the place. And she wanted to go back inside because she was cold in her pyjamas, and she only answered the door because she thought he was a delivery man bringing her a spicebag. They were still arguing when the cops pulled up behind him and he turned around in shock, with burnt eyebrows, wearing the jacket from the Polo. He couldn't believe it, *how*? The azure light of the law dancing on his moist pupils. Both doors opening, squawking radio. The melting end of short freedom. He blamed the ex-straight away for ringing them but she just closed the door and went back inside and lit a joint. He woke up the next morning again, back in jail, charged with more of the same as before and sure twas all the one. Great night out altogether.

All The Bad News On The Radio

Wasn't even sure if I wanted to go but fuck it, here I was. Party scene, mostly shitehawks on phones and smoking weed. Drink around, upturned ashtrays, candles burning in empty cheap wine bottles and a smell like melting butter, and old leather, and cartoons on the telly. And now it's time to go and I'm giving the lift home to a few but there's no stir, all talk, be ready in five minutes, and all that.

Then I remembered I was in the same estate yesterday. Sitting in the car, listening to all the bad news on the radio, when a man hobbled by.

So I asked the girl there: 'Do you know a fella around here, walks funny, saw him yesterday.'

Yeah, she said, that's Mike.

'Mike?'

Yeah, she said, lives next door. He has *problems.*

And then I knew I was right. That it

was him and the years hadn't been good. And I thought of the days gone by. Before the world crumbled, back when mystery was still a thing, and life hung on friendships and intuition, and knowing one of your own. He was a journalist, looking to get into the fiction game. Smart mind, good with people, knew how things worked. Ten years ago, fifteen now, who knows? Last time I saw him we had a session before I hit the road. Did the town. Places around Galway that are long closed since. Johnny Cash was only after dying and everyone was singing *Folsom Prison Blues,* like they were big fans, and then time went on. Different countries, different lives, different dead celebrities for new generations.

Girl here now is making a mention of things. Has that pitch of the pop psychologist. Joint in one hand, cheap can in the other, gives her incisive diagnosis. Alcoholism? Drugs maybe? I think it could be schizophrenia? He shouts a lot. Keeps locking the door, then opening it again, then locking it again. Some days it looks like he can't walk properly, others that he can. Talks to himself. Always shaking, tremors, nerves, something. Most people walk by in disgust, fear, nervous misunderstanding. Sad really, she says, but a nightmare to live beside.

And yet there was a time when his hands didn't shake and his mouth didn't quiver and his walk didn't slope and he was going to be a writer. Had met plenty through working with the papers and the material was there, somewhere in his mind, beyond the Galway rain and the cold cider, behind those eyes that hovered on the ledge of sanity. And there'd been a girl somewhere. A daughter maybe, a lover, some story of love and loss. He was working through it at the time, waiting for the cloud to pass and age to do her thing and find the level where they could work it out. Maybe settle down, maybe try again. Maybe find a room where the world could quieten and he could let the demons sing, purge them on a page, lit by the warm sun of peace and possibility. Listen to the laughter of life downstairs and leave the horror locked in the written words and it would all be ok.

Girl here now says she doesn't like him. Nobody does. He has a housemate that wants to move out. Or him to move out. Or something. He should really be *put somewhere*, she says, sent somewhere, some home, some place, somewhere else.

He'd lost weight too. Thin now, delicate musculature, imminently breakable. Acne, stubble, torn shoes and rotting teeth. And I remembered that night, before I left, we were outside a pub at some unholy hour. There was mongs selling cheap wine on the street, and a flavour of pizza in the air from Monroe's pub across the road. Style and opulence glittered at the taxi rank, looking for the next lift to nowhere. I had a flight in a few hours and I said to Mike I'd be in touch, and I'd see him around, and good luck with the writing. Sound, he said, and I'll catch you when you're home and we'll have a pint and we'll compare stories. And we shook hands and he left and I hadn't seen him since. Until now.

.

Lola Galway

Stephen packed up the books and left. He had been in college all day. It was exam time and there was stressed out students everywhere. He had had enough. His eyes were sore, he was hungry, and he was tired, and he was due to spend time with his girlfriend, Tanya. He put on his blue jacket and walked down the stairs towards the exit. His bag was heavy, and he thought about going to his locker to offload some of the weight.

Outside, there was a drizzle and other students stood chatting and smoking against the library wall. A lad with a clipboard was wandering around asking questions. Probably a survey about campus lifestyles or a petition against the current war. Stephen avoided him and made for the front gate, zipping up his jacket against the cold.

Dark fell on the evening, like an unwelcome friend. Cars zoomed up and down the road, making a splash as they hit the puddles by the footpath. He noticed a man on a bike with his hand out, indicating a right turn. Suddenly there was a squeal of brakes as a red Ford Mondeo swerved and narrowly missed him before screeching to a halt. Pause goes the world through the dying decibels and scent of burning rubber. The cyclist stopped, staring expectantly. He had a long coat, down to his ankles, and his gloved hands gripped the brakes. He watched the stalled car through narrow eyes, his grey stubbled face was deadpan. Stephen walked up and asked: 'Are you alright?'

Dublin accent, looked like a man called Linus, said: 'Fine thanks, lucky.'

'I saw you indicate. It wasn't your fault.'

'Pity you weren't driving.'

'Well, at least there was nobody hurt.'

'Yet.'

The driver was out now, hazard lights on, chest exposed through his partially open shirt and his belt buckle sparkling in the streetlight. His heavy boots thumped like an approaching army. He looked like a Mike, but pronounced *Mykke.* He opened, pure rural bollix, with: 'Ya prick. Ya fuckin prick. What d'ya think you're at?'

'Trying to turn right.'

'Ya stupid prick. You'd think you'd stay at home with your crock of shite and leave the road to the people with cars.'

'Look, I indicated, I have a right to be on the road as much as you.'

'Ah piss off. Yourself and your fuckin dynamos. Ye should all be locked up for obstruction.'

Stephen interjected. 'Hey, I saw it all and you were driving like a lunatic.'

He noticed Stephen for the first time, fired

up some menace and asked: 'Were you cycling the bike?'

'No.'

'Were ya driving the car?'

'No.'

'Well keep your fuckin nose outta business that's not yours then. Fuckin hippy students never did a day's work in their lives.'

Linus said: 'You nearly killed me because you were speeding. I put out my hand to indicate. In a court of law...'

'Court is it? I'll give ya *court*. Court's not for pain in the hole pedal pushers. I'll tell ya that much. Try some GBH, and you might be a bit closer...'

'That a threat?' asked Stephen.

'If there's so much as a scratch anywhere on that car, or if I think the steering is off, or if I find the tires are a bit worn down, there'll be bones broken. That much I can *guarantee*, and all the courts in the country won't help ye.'

Stephen shifted a bit, but Linus stayed firm and said: 'I'm getting a bit sick of you now.'

'What?' Said *Mykke*, as he moved closer. '*What* you say?'

Stephen got a whiff of his aftershave. Strong, fruity, cheap. Linus continued. 'I said, *I'm getting a bit sick of you now*. If ya can't drive properly you shouldn't be in a car. It's cowboys like you that are causing all the carnage on the roads.'

'Look, maybe we should go...' said Stephen.

'We're not going anywhere.'

'You reckon *I'm* causing the carnage? I should've run ya down when I had the chance, better luck next time I suppose.' He looked at Stephen. 'And you're no better, another useless prick. Two of ye should count your lucky stars I'm in a hurry tonight.'

He turned and walked to the car, situation almost diffused, hardly worth writing about until Linus shouted: 'Ye rednecks are *all talk*.'

Mykke, unexpectedly agile, was back in half a second, apoplectic, swung a haymaker and hit Linus in the jaw. There was a sound like breaking eggs and Linus gave no more resistance than a newspaper wall, pulling the bike back with him. Now he's on the ground, his body limp under a mess of handlebars and brake cables and twisted wheels.

'Get up ya bastard! Get up and I'll give ya more, come on!' *Mykke* gave him a hard kick to the ribs. 'Come on, let's see ya cycle your *ball of shite bike* after that.'

Stephen, numb with shock until now, jumped at *Mykke* and they got into a struggle, rolling over on the wet tarmac, trying to punch each other, but too close to cause any harm. Another car came on the scene and a man got out. Late forties, shirt and tie, air of authority, maybe some kind of a guard. Let's find out.

'Hey, hey, hey, break it up! Break it up! Come on!'

He pulled them apart and asked: 'What's the story here?'

'This bollix...' Said *Mykke*. 'Won't mind his own business. I was talkin to your man here and the next thing he comes over stickin his nose in, before I knew it he was trying to rob the bike and I was tryin to stop him.'

'That's a lie!' roared Stephen. 'Tell the truth.'

'That *is* the truth.'

'I think the best thing to do now is look after the man on the ground. Ye can sort out your differences later.'

The peacemaker, looked like an *Ollie*, bent down, blue eyes, tight haircut, looking curious for a second, said: 'Doesn't look too good, lads.' He checked the pulse, said: 'Not too good at all. In fact, I'd say one of ye heroes is in a bit of shit.'

'What're you talkin about?' Asked *Mykke*.

'I'm saying there's a dead man lying on the road. That make it any clearer for you? I'm a doctor. I should know.'

Stephen put his head in his hands, said: 'Oh, Jesus.'

Doctor Ollie checked the pockets for identification. He found a round box of medication. 'Let me see, Lipostat and Betaloc, Angina meds. Looks like a severe case.'

'You're fucked now.' Said *Mykke*, turning to Stephen.

'What?'

'Bad enough trying to rob him, but now

you're after killing him.'

'What are you talking about? *You* hit him and killed him. Tell him, it was *you*.'

'Fraid not, scan. Not takin this hit, no fuckin way. I have enough problems. Serves ya right for stickin your nose in.'

Ollie stood up, black pants, brown shoes, Hugo Boss, took control and said: 'I think it's time to make a few phone calls.'

The ambulance arrived, green outfits, facemasks and white gloves, defibrillators, sirens and horrified mouths in passing traffic. Linus was pronounced dead and clattered into the back on a steel bed. Stephen, Doctor Ollie, and Iron *Mykke* were brought to the station. White walls there, busy hands with biros, warm smell of printer ink, like a hospital for invisible diseases. *Mykke* explained that he and Linus had been *discussing* the incident on the road when Stephen tried to grab the bike. Stephen hit Linus – explained the *shaken Mykke* – and when *he* protested, Stephen jumped and knocked him to the ground. The collaboration of the doctor's statement was enough to justify a trial. Six months later, Stephen was convicted. Taking account of his age and educational pursuits, he got a three-year suspended sentence. Tanya left him. The case made the papers. The college didn't want him anymore. He went working on a building site, got drunk one Friday evening and crashed his car. A Ford Mondeo. This activated the sentence and they brought him straight to Castlerea prison. He's been there ever since. Wondering where it all went wrong.

*

Stephen packed up the books and left. He had been in college all day. It was exam time and there was stressed out students everywhere. He had had enough. His eyes were sore, he was hungry, and he was tired, and he was due to spend time with his girlfriend, Tanya. He put on his blue jacket and walked down the stairs towards the exit.

Outside, there was a drizzle and other students stood chatting and smoking against the library wall. A lad with a clipboard was wandering around asking questions. Probably a survey about campus lifestyles or a petition against the current war.

Stephen's bag was heavy, and he decided to go to his locker and drop off some books. He met Brian on the way. Leather jacket, blue jeans, Lynx Africa, gelled hair in the orange lamplight. Ready for a night out.

'Howya, Steve?'

'How's Brian?'

'Not too bad. Comin for a beer?'

'Ah, dunno man, have a lotta work to do. Ya goin *out* out or just out?'

'See what happens. Fuck it, ya need a break. Come on.'

There was a screech of tires in the distance.

'Da fuck is that?' Asked Brian.

Stephen shrugged, said: 'I was thinkin of headin out to Tanya's place. Haven't seen her in a while.'

'Sure you could have *the one* and head out after?'

'Right sure, fuck it. I'll just put my bag in the locker and meet ye down there.'

'Sound job.'

Brian went. Stephen dialled Tanya's number. She answered and he said: 'Alright, babe?

'Heya, still at the library?'

'Yeah, yeah, well… technically.'

'Technically?'

'Well…finished in the library, but still at the college.'

'Oh cool, so you're on the way out to me?'

'Might just go for a chat with Brian and head out then.'

'By *chat* you mean *pint?*'

'Probably.'

'Steve?'

'Wha?'

'We haven't spent time together in weeks.'

'We've been busy studying.'

'Don't play so innocent. You have a choice between me and the lads and you're pickin *the lads*.'

'It's just for one. I'll call out when I'm finished.'

'When you're pissed off your tits? Don't

bother.'

Click.

He called her back. She didn't answer.

Later at the bar.

'Two pints,' ordered Brian and turned to Stephen. 'Did you tell herself?'

'Yeah, she was pure thick. I'm not stayin long.'

'Famous last words.'

Brian spotted something, curious *into the distance* look, said: 'Hey, ya know that one from the politics tutorial?'

'Which one?'

'Babe, sits up the front.'

'Blonde?'

'That's her over there. *Karen* is her name. Come on, we're goin over.'

Stephen saw her now too. Short black dress, tights, knee high boots, straight blonde hair. He remembered her as sharp, smart, but vaguely wild, energy he couldn't fathom, like she knew him better than he knew himself.

Karen saw them coming, said: 'Stephen!'

'Karen, how are you?'

'Absolutely sloshed. I'm here since three.' She thought for a second and pointed at Brian. 'Barry? Hang on, hang on, Brendan? No, Boris? Bart?'

'Brian.'

'Oh yeah, sorry.' She giggled, then leaned over the side of her chair and used Stephen for support. Beige painted perfect nails, erotic perfume, like the real dear stuff in *Boots*. Her touch infected him with desire and he tried to ignore it, like a priest's battle with celibacy. She said: 'It's my round guys, what do ye want?'

'No, I'm fine, I'm going home.' Said Stephen.

'No, you're not. You're having a drink.'

Convincing nobody, least of all himself, he said: 'No, honestly, Karen. I'm ok.'

She slurred, then hiccupped, perfect teeth, shiny glossed lips. 'Stephen...I'll be very insulted if you just go home. I *insist* you have a drink with me.'

He swirled his pint around. 'Well, suppose I could have one more.'

Six pints later, they were caught in the whirlwind of *the round.* The craic was going good, doing her thing, singing the song of sweet memories to be. Stephen asked: 'Brian? Guinness again, yeah?'

'Nah, I'll just have a shot before the club.'

'Club?'

'Well I'm not gonna have a feed pints and just go home.'

'Tanya's goin to kill me.'

'Is she the girl that always wears the tracksuits?' Asked Karen.

'If you're goin to do somethin wrong, do it right. Mine's a vodka.' Said Brian.

He went outside to call Tanya, got her voicemail and slurred into the phone. 'Yeah listen,

Tanya. It's me, ya? Stephen ya? Just callin bout the…'

The man with the clipboard saw Stephen and walked over. He was about the same age, white jacket, red runners, his face obscured by a baseball cap. He tapped the biro lightly, said: 'Excuse me.'

Stephen hung up, said: 'Yeah?'

'I was wondering if you could help me with something.'

'Ah, I'm a bit busy.'

'It's just two questions.'

'Just two?'

'Yeah, honestly.'

'Ok, quick then, come on.'

'Well, number one: Is this a novel or a short story?'

'Am… short story I think, getting a bit dragged out now though. Still, *short story*.'

'Thank you and how many words are we on?'

'2204.'

'Including these?'

'No.'

'And are you the main character?'

'That's four questions.'

'Just answer and I'll leave you alone.'

'Am yeah, think so, well… it's all about me, isn't it?'

'Thanks, Stephen. I'll call ahead and try get it wrapped up fast. Can you sign here please?'

'Cheers, no problem.'

He signed.

'Brilliant, thanks again. That's all for now.'

Stephen walked back into the bar and ordered the vodkas. In the morning, he woke up in Karen Murphy's bed, delighted with himself. Five years later they got married and Brian was the best man and told the story at the wedding about how Stephen nearly didn't come out that night and how different it all might have been.

*

Stephen packed up the books and left. He had been in college all day. It was exam time and there was stressed out students everywhere. He had had enough. His eyes were sore, he was hungry, and he was tired, and he was due to spend time with his girlfriend, Tanya. He put on his blue jacket and walked down the stairs towards the exit.

Outside, there was a drizzle and other students stood chatting and smoking against the library wall. A lad with a clipboard was wandering around asking questions. Probably a survey about campus lifestyles or a petition against the current war. Stephen's bag was heavy, and he decided to drop some books at his locker. He searched for his phone to call Tanya as he walked and realized he had left it on the desk. He went back to get it and called her on the way out.

She answered, he said: 'Alright, Babe?'

'Heya, still at the library?'

'Nah, just left. Dropping some stuff in my locker. What're you up to?'

'Tryin to study. What's your plan for the night?'

'At a bit of a loose end, you?

'Nah...nothing.'

'Feel like watching a film?'

Brian walked by, all dressed up, and saluted Stephen. He waved back. Tanya said: 'Film sounds good. Do you want to start walking out?'

'Yeah. See ya in twenty minutes?'

'Cool, I'll put the fire on. It's freezing out here.'

He got to his locker and the phone rang. It was Brian. He said: 'Alright,man?'

'Howya, Brian. What's the craic?

'Not a lot. Comin for a beer?'

'Nah, just called Tanya there, heading out to her place and goin watchin a film'

'Can't tempt ya for just the one pint, no?'

'Thanks, but not tonight. After the exams maybe?'

'Sound, no bother, cheers anyway, enjoy the flick.'

He left through the front gate. There was a stalled car on the road. The driver door hanging open, hazard lights on. Two men, one holding a bike, were arguing on the path. Another car pulled up and a third man got out and tried to calm them down.

Stephen left them to it and kept going.

Tanya's house was at the back of an estate, just off the city centre. He walked through, keeping an eye on the door numbers. All the buildings looked the same, closed curtains and nice gardens.

Next thing he heard a loud thud coming from one of the driveways and he heard a voice muttering. He looked but couldn't see anyone. He walked over to investigate, and a man sprang up from the grass and said: 'How's it goin?'

Stephen was slightly shocked, but more curious. 'Hi, you ok?'

'Yeah, fine thanks. Just a bit of a rough journey.'

'You were travelling?'

'Yeah. Never gets easy, all this story hopping. You must be Stephen?'

'I am.'

He brushed some grass from his dishevelled suit, his bright eyes dancing with a piercing energy.

'Where you off to, Steve?'

'Tanya's place.'

'How's that goin?'

'Not too bad.'

'Good stuff.'

'And what are *you* at? Fallin in on a story like this? It's a bit pointless, isn't it?'

'Who're ya tellin? Your man with the clipboard's gone on the piss, drooling over some burd at the college, Karen someone. I don't know.'

'The dodge.'

'Yeah, first he met some fella called Boris who brought him for a pint and sure it all went wrong from there.'

'Why's your suit so dirty?'

'Slept in it for the last three days. Called back from a mighty wedding in Mayo for this.'

'Where was the weddin on?'

'Ballinrobe, buncha lunatics.'

He pulled a notebook and pencil from his pocket.

'Right. This still a short story?'

'Ah, yeah, comin near the end now I think.'

'Fuckin want to be. How many words are we on?'

'2980.'

'Including these?'

'No.'

He scribbled something and looked up. 'Now, that's that sorted. This is Forster Court, isn't it?'

'Yeah, you lookin for somewhere?'

'102. There's a fella goin out cycling a bike and I want to tell him to stay in cos his heart's not great. Hope I'm not too late.'

Stephen pointed towards an alleyway. 'Straight up through there and it's about the seventh house on your left I think.'

'Good man, yourself. You'll stay in for the night now, ya will?'

'Probably, yeah.'

'Not too bad. Tell ya what though, ya better

run.'

'Why?'

'Just that I think they were on about wrappin this one up fast, on account of the words and that, and you'd want to get up to the woman's house before it's finished or you'll be caught out here with me, you know?'

'Oh fuck.'

'Oh no, jez, don't get me wrong, ya seem like a nice fella, it's just that it's not that much craic really, and sometimes a story ending might never get fixed up and your stuck then altogether just wandering around the place.'

'Sound, I'll keep goin so.'

'G'luck.'

Tanya sat watching television. She was sick of studying and she was looking forward to seeing Stephen. The doorbell rang. He kissed her as he walked in. She said: 'Took your time, fire's nearly gone down.'

'Sorry, got caught talking to a fella out there.'

'Come in and keep me warm.'

Inside, she fixed up the couch with duvets and cushions and got the telly ready to go.

'Nothing strange tonight?' She asked.

'Nah, usual library craic. Quiet enough for you here?'

'Yeah, I hate that place around exam time.'

'We shoulda got popcorn.'

'Or wine.'
'How many words we on?'
'3272.'
'Including these?'
'No.'
'I'm glad you made it.'
'Me too.'
'Right film's on…Shhss.'

Train Drama

There was a black girl at the station and she didn't know how to use the ticket machine. Sunday evening, offices closed, figure it out. She went up to the steward at the door and asked him for help. He was white Irish, midlands thick. Always up for being contrary, looking for the fight, thinks he's Steven Segal and the place might be under attack. He looked at her suspicious, like she might be some kind of scam, herself and her dreads, and the tight black jeans, and the leather jacket. It all gave him visions of dangerous Voodoo rituals involving dangerous snakes. He listened, incredulous, then shook his head and said he couldn't help her and it wasn't his job anyway. He was just there to mind the door.

So she went back to pressing buttons. It was all nonsense. She went on the phone, tried something online, made no headway there. She approached the other passengers, all Europeans with the latest earphones, and they didn't want to know. Too many emails from Nigerian princes, too many lost promises of gold bars, they'd heard it all before. Eventually she went back to your man again, said: 'Please, you *work* here. I need your help.'

He gave her the up and down again, saw demonic incantations, deadly potions in hieroglyphic pots out foreign, where they lived in galvanize huts and shared the bed with goats. He said: 'I'm not here to help *you*.'

'Can you please tell me how to buy a ticket?'

'No. And you're not gettin on the train without one.'

A second lad came along. Wiry. Security badge on his arm. A name like Estefan. Cold eyes. Delighted there was some action. He crowded her, asked: 'What's the problem here?'

Segal said: 'Has no ticket.'

'No ticket?'

'Nothin.'

She got nervous, said: 'I just don't know how to use the machine.'

'It's over there.' Said Estefan, the same way you tell a dog to go outside.

'I know, but I need you to help me.'

'Why would we help *you*?'

'Because you work here, and I don't know what I'm doing.'

Segal huffed. Estefan thought of something, reached into his pocket and pulled out a facemask. Made a big deal of putting it on, made sure it was tight, effective. He leaned in a bit closer, but not enough to get infected, said: 'Where you goin?'

'Dublin. I need to see my child and I can't miss the train.'

'Well you won't be comin through here without a ticket.'

She sighed, backed away a bit, wondered, then said: 'How bout this – I get on the train and I buy from somebody on there?'

Segal rolled his eyes. Estefan stood at the door, arms folded, legs apart, looking like a Ninja, said: 'You're not goin anywhere.'

Noise stage left, a door squeals, enter a third employee, wearing a high viz vest with the company logo and name on the back. Had the look of someone with authority and experience in customer service, maybe even conflict resolution. He walked over, glasses, belly, purple tie, asked: 'What's the problem here?'

She spoke first, relieved, said: 'I'm really sorry, but I can't use the machine and these two guys are refusing to help me, maybe it's my fault, call me lazy or whatever, but I just can't figure it out...'

High viz looked at her, saw social welfare fraud, stolen wallets on the train, possible solicitation of lonely farmers. He got caught himself one night the same way, out abroad with a *black wan*, marched to the ATM by her two pimps and cleaned, was never able to tell anyone. €300 they got for not so much as a *handjob* and he wasn't going falling for this kinda thing again. He raised his arms, said: 'I'm sorry, but if you're too lazy to bother gettin a ticket then you won't be gettin any help from anyone here. Now, that's the end of it.'

She started to protest but the train arrived. A heaving horse on the platform. Passengers with tickets walked out and started to board. Segal and Estefan stood like bouncers, watching her in case she made a dash. They were so concerned they barely paid any attention to the people with tickets. Just nodded them on with fraternal knowing.

I walked over, said to her: 'I'll show you how to do it.'

'Can you? *Please?*'

'C'mon.'

There, she gave me her visa card and pin number, said: 'Please just get me to Dublin City Centre so I can see my kid, that's all I want. I should sue this place.'

I found the right fare, bought it, and the ticket popped out. The train made noises like it was about to take off. I said: 'You better run.'

And she did. Segal made sure to take a good look on her way through. She said it was a disgrace what happened. He followed her all the way up the platform to the door of the carriage, shouting: 'It's not my job to be buying tickets for the *likesa you*. Do you think I've nothin better for doin?'

And then she was on, and the train was gone. After, all three stood around. Estefan, Segal, High Viz, said things like: 'Never again....shouldn't have to put up with that kinda thing from anyone...if she ever walks through that door again I'll make sure she's not allowed get a train from here. Who does she think she is?'

Counter Revolution

The pub was all go. Liberals at the bar, talking the woke code. Take *Joe*. Drives a delivery van all day and hates black people. Sees the problems first hand. Says they don't work and they're not Irish and why don't they go back to their own country? Mary down the back, drinking a snowball, shouts up that she agrees. John's just back from *The Wok Inn*, eating a 4-in-1 in the corner *(chips, curry, chicken, rice)*, treating himself after getting the dole, mutters to himself: 'And the fuckers don't pay tax either.'

Joe's on a roll now. Audience. Encouragement. Validation. Soon he's on to the news, and that woman that married a terrorist in the middle east. And how could we let her back into the country? She's obviously a terrorist too. Coming back in by stealth. Has a plan to kill us all. Even if not, did she not leave of her own free will? And it didn't work out so *fuck her*, let her die out there. Not our problem. Don't get me wrong, says Joe, it's just my opinion. Everyone's entitled to their opinion and this is mine. I'm Irish, he says, pay tax here. Contribute to society. Abides by the law and why am I paying for terrorists to come and go on government jets? He takes another drink. Silence. Then Paddy falls off the couch. He's been struggling for a while. Doing his best with a pint of stale Carlsberg but nobody noticed he'd fallen asleep. Everyone was transfixed by Joe and his apparent logic. But now Paddy's on the ground, splayed.

Someone asks: 'Alright there, Paddy?'

But he's too unconscious to answer. Two lads bend down, catch him under the arms. Up now, Paddy, good man. He's in a blue coat and moustache. Got the double dole today. Starting the Christmas in style. Joe says: 'There's a true Irishman for ya. Drinks his pints as they come.'

Meanwhile the jukebox kicks off. Guns 'n Roses. *Right next door to hell.* It's loud and doesn't suit the relative emptiness. And Joe's annoyed cos he can't be heard. Paddy gets put back on the couch but he's still asleep and doesn't even know he fell. They set him up in a safe way so he's much further from the edge and won't fall again. Then they tilt his head back and leave his pint in front of him so it'll be right there when he wakes up.

The music stops. Joe's ready to bounce off the walls again with: 'I can't stand that Valkazar bastard.'

'Why not?' Asks a voice down the back.

'He's a Russian bastard.' Says Joe.

He's not Russian, says the voice, at least she doesn't think he is. Someone else says they remember when he was elected and there was talk of him being Indian.

The barman says: 'No, he wasn't elected, the gays got him in and everyone was too afraid to say anything.'

'That's what I'm talking about.' Says Joe. 'Fuckin queer Indians runnin the place. John Wayne is what we need to come and wipe out the whole lot of them out. The blacks, the Indians, the terrorists, and the fudge packin bastards. They're not Irish. I pay tax here for a country that's full of sponging immigrants. Sure it's even run by a fuckin immigrant. So what hope have we?'

Man along the bar shouts: Bring on the next election!

Hup outta that! Chimes in another.

You know what, says Joe. 'We should set up our own political party. Irish people only. No foreigners. Well, Polish and that are ok. But none of the other fuckers.'

'What'll we call it?' Asks Mary.

'*Ireland First.* No Russians allowed. Or Pakies. Or Blacks. Or arse bandits. Just tax paying Irish and you know what?'

'What?'

'We'd fuckin clean up. I'd have the whole country sorted in a week.'

'Want another pint?' Asks the barman.

Fill it up ta fuck, says Joe, I'm only getting started here...

Rualie Bualie

There was a band starting in a while. *Rualie Buaile* they were called. *Supposed to be mighty.* Another couple landed beside us. Him with the tattoos and an orange T-shirt and a pint of lager. Her with the red wine, black hair and the pink painted nails.

Are these chairs taken, do you mind if we sit beside ye, where ye from?

We got talking.

Your man was six foot tall and nearly five foot wide.

Square measured head like the graphics off a Commodore 64.

We did the talk, filled the social silence with polite noise.

What do you do yourself? Are ye staying here? Was it a long drive?

Noise to the right, a fight breaking out at the bar. Two clowns pushing each other and a girl trying to break it up. Something about a joke gone wrong. What do you mean by that? I'll burst your head. And your one slurring: 'Leave it lads, leave it!' And she barely able to stand.

Commodore turned to me and said: 'Don't ever get involved, lad.'

'Heh?'

'Fights, I'll tell you, waste of time, take it from me...let them at it.'

'Why's that?'

'I'll tell ya why. I was outside *Supermacs* not so long ago... havin a smoke. Seen this fella arguin with his woman. She was wearin a big pink jacket, that's why I noticed her. She was tryin to walk away and he was pullin her back, and she was screamin at him, and next thing I know he hits her a box in the face and knocks her out clean cold.'

He slapped his palm with his fist and said: 'Bang!'

'Did ya intervene?'

'Yeah, so I threw my fag on the ground, and I went straight over to your man and I says *pick on someone your own size*! And I broke his jaw with a right hook.'

He stood up and mimicked the action here, a wide arc, swift, fast, muscular, full body weight behind it, hissed through his teeth with the imaginary blow. *Sisssss/fizz....*

I said: 'Broke it?'

He sat back down, excited now, like the opposite of PTSD, almost knocked his pint, dollops of lager jumping for safety to the floor. He grabbed the glass, drank what was left, rasped and said: 'Clean broke it. And two of his teeth fell out on the path and rolled down a drain. I felt bad about that alright, dentists are fuckin dear, but what can you do? He hit a woman.'

'What did ya do then? Go home?'

'No. Wait til ya hear this. What do you think happened?'

'I don't know.'

'Weren't the cops after landing behind me?'

'They were not?'

'They fuckin were, like the dawn of bad justice.'

'And they arrested ya?'

'On the spot. I put up my hands, says, *I don't mind, I'll do the time, he hit a woman, it was worth it. I'd do it again too. Bring me in lads….*'

'Did ya not explain to them what happened?'

'Yeah but sure *save it for the judge* they said.'

'How'd that go?'

'I'll tell ya how it went. There was a court case about six months later and they had me up for assault. *Grievous Bodily Harm*. And I wouldn't mind, but I've a few convictions already like, so it didn't really suit, but the judge was a woman and I was hopin she'd understand.'

'And did she?'

'No.'

'Why not?'

'Well, ask me who the first witness was, up to the stand, to testify against me?'

'Your man that you hit?'

'No. The girlfriend. Your one that he knocked out, that I was *protecting*. Stands up and says it was all my fault, they weren't arguin at all and I just came over and attacked them. Fuckin bitch.'

'Quare badness.'

'I'm fuckin tellin ya. And she wearin the same pink jacket. Nailed me to the cross. Stickin up for the bollox that was batein her.'

'What the judge say?

'Nine months. Suspended.'

'You were lucky.'

'That's what I mean, though. I'll tell ya, next woman I see gettin a box they can tap dance on her fuckin head for all I care, I'm not getting involved, waste of fuckin time...'

Supergirl

I was trying to write when she walked in. New neighbour, getting familiar with the natives. It was around three o'clock. Usually, she's drunk by now. Buys a bottle of Vodka every morning and has it mostly drank by the afternoon. Normally it's in a flask and she carries it around, pretends it's water, and drinks it casually as the hours pass. Today she wants to know what the music is, says it sounds familiar, she used to listen to it in Poland before she moved over.

She sat on the couch. Blue jeans, white blouse, her pale face mousesque under the curly black scattered hair. A scent like carbolic and lavender. I told her it was *Reamonn*, *Supergirl.* She loved that. It got her thinking, made her nostalgic, fall into her story, her sad background narrative, no encouragement needed, except maybe the bleak loneliness of the daytime drinker. Her blue eyes, her small mouth, her voice like the song of the addict's self-sympathy. She took a pull of the flask, said she used to drink a lot in Warsaw. Party girl. Young. Finding herself. Strobe lights in dark discos, dance beats and boys. Her new fella wanted to move to Ireland. Big money, better life. She mostly had the language and they liked to drink in Ireland too and it all sounded perfect.

So they packed up, moved over. That was ten years ago. She was twenty-eight at the time. Had two fast kids. Bought a house. She even had a job for a while but lost it. It was everyone's fault. The boss, the manager, the conditions, the hours, the pay. She was better than that, didn't need it, there's better things out there.

She drank some more, said: 'I really love this song.'

'*Supergirl*?'

'Yeah. We used to listen to it all the time at home.'

'Before you moved over?'

'Before....everything.'

She shimmied a bit, put a hand up to the beats. Took a drink, offered the flask, said: 'Want some?'

'I'm grand, thanks.'

The story continues. The kids are gone. The husband took them. She had her own apartment for a while but she didn't pay the rent (landlord's fault) and now that's gone aswell. These days she lives with my neighbour (73) and makes him dinner every evening and he gives her money for the off-licence. Lately he's getting annoyed because the dinner does be burnt and he's noticing things going missing around the house. First it was his mobile phone and she blamed the fella up the road. Then a jar of change and it must have been that woman that visited the day before. Then some real money went AWOL after he collected the pension and maybe it was a robbery? Might be time to call the guards? He's also the kind of the man to keep a suitcase of cash under the bed. He went looking for it yesterday to buy a car and sure most of it was gone. Had vanished. Disappeared.

'Poof!' She said, like a teary-eyed magician.

And it's all a bit mixed up at the moment so she's giving him some space and hanging out here, listening to *Supergirl*. And where did I get the computer? It's really nice. And do I like this town? And was I ever in Poland? It's good, but Ireland is better. Much better. She wants to see her kids at the weekend but the husband won't let her. Won't answer the phone. Last time she got too drunk (his fault) and didn't show up and there's been no word since. But she has a plan. There's going to be a court day soon, solicitors, a real showdown, she's got it all planned as she enjoys the song some more, hums along, transformed back to the careless place, takes another swig and feels invincible. A real *Supergirl.*

The Commute

Mystic light in the November dawn. We have an aerial shot of the bus driver in a navy jumper and black pants. His name is Mattie. Beetroot face and flabby jowls. A real morning oracle, champion of the commuter elite. Let's zoom in as he looks at the couple with the guide-dog and says: 'I'm sorry, but you can't bring *that* on.'

'*Excuse me*?' Said the woman. She was in a long black dress, green eyes and an earthy disposition. Had her hair tied back with something bright blue. Her bag was the colour of the rainbow.

'Not a notion, forget about it, no. No way. I'll have to ask your friend to leave the animal behind.'

The other commuters slowed and stared as they boarded. Their observations asking: Is this a climate thing? Protestors? Hippies? Christ it's not *Pride* already, is it?

'But, why?' Protested the woman. 'It's not as if it's a pet. It's a *guide-dog.*'

'I understand that missus, but the boss'll kill me if he finds dogs on the bus. Sure he'll go mad.'

'Yes, but...'

'And the other passengers too....what about them?'

'What do you mean?'

Exasperated wave of his hands here. 'Well, what if the dog does its business inside? What happens then? People complain and we're all out of the job.'

'I'm aware of that, but this is a highly trained *guide.* They're not like other animals. There must be *something* you can do? I mean, we really need to get to the city today. It's for a medical appointment. Is what you're saying even *legal*?'

Mattie got nervous here. She was getting dirty now. He looked at his watch.

'Look, I'll ring the boss. If he says it's ok, then it's ok, ok?'

'Yes, ok, thank you.'

He did the phone thing, out of earshot. Now the bus is full. Everyone staring out from inside, waiting for the invisible hand of civilized society to crush this rogue interruption. After all, it was getting late. A light breeze blew, like the whisper of the morning slipping away. Brighter now, the sun waiting for nobody. And the blind man fared no better in civil expectations. Long black hair down to the elbows of his denim jacket. Dark glasses, holding the leash for the dog. They all looked on, forming diverse impressions. Up from the drug infested council estate? An unknown quantity from Eastern Europe? AIDS? Christ, what if they blow up the bus?

Mattie was still talking as he walked back. Maybe he thought the couple was deaf because he was saying: 'Yeah, yeah, I know what you mean, yeah, that's exactly what I said. Fuck them. Let them get a taxi. I'll tell them that now. People wouldn't like it anyway. Okay...'

He listened.

'Will do.'

Listened more.

'No bother, Tom. Okay, bye, bye, bye.'

He hung up, returned and shrugged.

'I'm sorry, but there's nothin I can do. I rang himself there now and he says it's against regulations to have animals on the bus. I'd love to help ye, but it's just out of my hands. That order came straight from the top. If it was up to me, there'd be no problem, but, unfortunately, rules are rules.'

He took out his wallet, found a business card.

'Here's the number of a taxi. Give them a call and they might be able to help ye. There's nothin I can do. Like I said, it's out of my hands.'

She took the card, said: 'But, we can't afford this. That's why we're getting the bus. Surely there's an exception for the blind?'

He shrugged again.

'Ring *head office* if ye like. I'll have to go now coz of the thraffic. There's people waiting to go to work. *Ye* might have all day for talkin but *we* don't.'

He hopped in. An experienced *hopped inner*.

The shape of his arse folding into the seat. He turned the ignition and took the roar of the engine personal, like it was in a hurry. He pressed a button and the door closed slowly, hissing like a snake's warning, and then the bus was gone.

The dog stood up, alert at the activity. The woman looked at the business card.

It's not far, she said. *We can walk.*

-

The rain, like rubber pellets, bounced off the windshield as Mattie changed gears, formula one style, and looked at his watch.

'Half the fuckin mornin gone with them...' He muttered.

'What was the story with them freaks outside?' Asked a woman from behind. We'll call her Sheila. She looks like a Shelia. The bitchy type. Black pants, flat shoes, curly black hair. Getting married next year, like respectable people are supposed to do.

He replied through the mirror. 'Did ya spot them, ya did?'

'Yeah, hard to miss. What they want? A free lift or somethin? Or were they beggin?'

'Wanted to bring the fuckin dog on the bus! Dogs like, on the bus!'

'WHA...? Were they actually serious?'

'Yeah, and I sez, what the fuck do ya think I am? Does this look like some sort of a pet shop? Or a shaggin zoo or somethin?'

'Jesus, on the bus? I can't *stand* dogs.'

'Me neither, 'n I sez that too, I sez, you think the ordinary decent workin folk are gonna put up with that, the likes of ye comin in with animals? Puttin piss and shit and every sorta fuckin thing all over the floor? Who'll clean it up then? When they're bollickin around the city? I sez, d'ya think I've nothin' better for doin?'

'You were dead right, let them get a taxi. They looked half stoned anyway.'

'Fuckin right, sure half them crowd with the long hair are all on the drugs anyway. Stoned as fuckin bags at half seven in the mornin. They can piss off now and find their own way.'

'And come here to me, will you not get in trouble now? Like, if they ring up complainin or somethin?'

'Nah. I sez, hang on an' I'll ring the boss now, and I goes around the corner like, so they couldn't hear what I'd been sayin, ya know? They're the type of cute cunts that'd be listenin when you're on the phone, ya know yourself?'

'Know what ya mean, yeah.'

'So I goes around an' I rang like. And he answers an' I sez, *Tom*? Now, it's Monday mornin and Tom doesn't like to be disturbed on the best of mornin's, you know the craic yourself. And I sez, *Tom*? There's a crowd of quare lookin bastards here that want to go bringing dogs to Galway....and he sez for fuck sake, Mattie, what're ya ringin *me* for?

And I sez, just in case, because of the *disincremation* crowd and all that ya know? They're tryin to say one of them is *blind* like.'

He switched the wipers from slow to fast and the engine surged as he changed gears again. The heating kicked in now, everyone in a warm safe capsule, no more social hiccups.

'So Tom sez, he sez, what're ya on about, Mattie? And I told him the shtory again and he sez, he sez, – will ya ever fuck off, and tell them YOKES, that if they think they're goin bringin dirty bastardsa dogs on my bus they can go shove them where the sun don't definitely shine.'

He let the joke settle, she gave a sympathetic chuckle.

'And then he sez, he sez, wait until ya hear this now, he asks: Are they knacks like? Cousins? And I sez no, *stoned lookin fuckers*, and sure he went cracked then entirely. Out ta fuck with them! Jesus Christ, he sez, get rid of them fasht! For the love 'n honour a God, and I sez, that's exactly what I said....ya know?'

'Proper order.'

'Next thing he asks, was I still in town? An I sez I was and he sez get your hole on the road or you'll be stuck in thraffic all mornin! So I hung up and told them the way it was and gave them a number for a taxi. Your wan was getting a bit emotional alright but, fuck her, not my problem.'

'Not yours or mine or anyone else's either, that's for sure. And you wouldn't see me on no bus with dogs.'

She crossed her legs. Adamant like. Did something with her hair. Pulled it back, tied it. The engagement ring glitters.

'Or me drivin it. The likes of that kinda carry on now makes me sick. Dirty bastards. You'd think the guards'd be able to do somethin about them type now? Hangin around like that, causin trouble and holdin people up, sure just look at the time it is.'

'Ridiculous. They didn't even look Irish.'

'They'll spend the resht of the day now in the dole office I suppose, lookin for handouts to pay for a taxi...'

He pressed hard on the pedal. There'd be school traffic soon. Pure crustaceans on the combustion food chain, paralyzing the city with their family act. That's the last thing we want, and with the rain too? *Drive her on. Drive her on. Drive her on.*

He took a corner too wide and was flashed by an Audi.

Another passenger came up from the aisle.

Suit, spiky hair, Wall Street Mayo job.

Prick.

'Are we going to be late coz of them druggies?'

'My knob we'll be late,' said Mattie Luther King.

'But what about the traffic, we'll hardly beat it now? Look at the time. We'll hit a tailback in another five miles.'

'Not if I can help it.'

'You sure?'

He nodded.

'What they want anyway? Environmental shite, was it?'

'Refugees,' said Sheila. 'Parasites looking for sympathy.'

'I'm not sure,' said Mattie. 'But I didn't like the look of the blind lad. Could be a scam too, have the whole bus robbed before we know it. What'll Tom say then?'

'Or one of them might have a convenient fall,' says Shelia. 'Probably looking for a handy compensation claim...'

'I thought it was some kind of gay pride thing.'

'Oh, worse again,' says Mattie. 'Sure ya wouldn't know are half of *them* men or women.'

'Sick.' Said Sheila.

Gordon Gecko went back and announced to everyone they were still on schedule. There was collective relief. Capitalism was winning.

The rain beat harder, lashing the huskies up the road. Everything looking like a blurry photograph through the bus windows.

They got to Ballindooley, a few miles outside. Almost made shite of a black Dacia doing the school run. Had to break hard, skid a bit. Heads jerked forward and moaned and groaned. The audacity of the bus, the inconvenient tarmac, the cheek of the weather, these other useless road users, who do we complain to?

Mattie eased around the next bend, ready to floor it again, get around the Dacia. Then he looked ahead in horror as the new picture emerged. An unthinkable thing. An apocalyptic line of cars, going nowhere. Nowhere at all. Not even moving a small bit. Welded to the road. He pounded the steering wheel, cursing to himself. Tension descended like a slow puncture.

'I thought you said you could make it?' Said Sheila, finding her inner shrill. 'I thought you said we wouldn't be late?'

'What I said was, not if I can help it. I couldn't help it. What can I do?'

'Feck that. Overtake someone. C'mon, I can't be late. It'll hold up the whole shift.'

'Sure what the fuck can I do?'

'Blow the horn, be aggressive.' She stood up and reached in to press it herself. Handy act as she was in the front seat of the bus, ready to be the first off, steal seconds from the losers. But now she tripped a bit and stumbled into Mattie, her breasts in his face. Pure burlesque gone wrong. He pushed her away.

'Go way and sit down! I'll do the drivin and the beepin, get away.'

Shelia sat down, adjusting her bra, mortified. But furious too. Seething at the lack of obedience when demanded. A caution to all unsuspecting photographers, cakemakers and wedding bands.

Someone shouted up from the back: 'It's your fault, you could've just let them dirtbags on and we'd have made it.'

He turned around, astonished.

'Yeah,' said another passenger. 'Why didn't ya just let them on? What were you doin out there for twenty minutes?'

There was a murmur of approval from the back.

Mattie waved his hand in dismissal. 'Aragh, piss off.'

Sheila had the phone out now, explaining to someone that she was going to be late, and how *her driver* was a pervert.

Mattie turned on the radio, trying to block it all out. The news came on. There was a killing in Dublin and a robbery in Athenry. Politicians were on defending a new pay rise they gave themselves.

The passengers looked out into the rain-drenched fields. The cars in front inched slowly forward now but suddenly there was a bulletin. A sense of urgency in the reporter's voice.

'Turn it up!' Shouted the wank in the suit.

Mattie obliged, anything to keep the fuckers quiet.

'....and news just in. All those travelling to Galway should avoid the Headford Road as there's been a collision which has caused a massive tailback and traffic in and out of the city will be severely congested for the rest of the morning. Motorists are *advised to take alternative routes or expect up to a delay of up to three hours...*

Mattie slumped over the wheel and pressed his head into his elbows, bobbing it up and down.

'Fuck, fuck, fuck.'

Paddy Backs Ruby Walsh At The Galway Races

We were working for the races. Doing security. Checking tickets for the VIP stadium where you had the best view of the track. Paddy was at the bottom door, an eccentric mid-fifties, grey hair and a voice like soft bread.

He opened with: 'Hey, Micky…?'

'Yeah, Paddy?'

'Was there many here last night?'

'A good few.'

'A good few?'

'Yeah.'

'A few thousand I suppose?'

'Around that, yeah.'

'Around that. Ok. What time was the last race?'

'Eight or so.'

'Did you back any horses?'

'No, Paddy, we're not supposed to bet when we're working.'

'Oh, yeah, oh yeah.'

A rich couple walked up. His suit, her feather hat, she asked: 'Where do I go?'

'Where do you want to go?'

'Well...' she said: '*Here*?'

'Ok, upstairs or downstairs?'

She produced a ticket and said: 'What does this say?'

I read it, went: 'You're in the wrong building.'

She revved all her wealthy horsepower and said: 'No, we're not. Sheila said to come here.'

'Who's Sheila?'

'She organised it.'

'Organised what?'

'The dinner.'

Your man chimed in then, with: 'We're here for the dinner with Sheila.'

'Well you have tickets for the other side of the stadium.'

'The OTHER side?' She said. 'But Sheila said to come here.'

'Sheila was wrong.'

'Excuse me?'

Your man had the phone out now. Getting to the bottom of *this*.Three underage lads came along, stupid haircuts, dressed like the Peaky Blinders. They went for the door. I stopped them with a hand and said: 'Tickets?'

They all said together: 'Tickets?'

'Yeah.'

'Oh.'

And they disappeared. Meanwhile, the husband was back and said: 'Sheila said we're to go across to the other side.'

'This is ridiculous.' Said the feather lady.

'I'd hate to see this place if there was a fire.' Said your man.

And off they went. Paddy was waiting patiently at his door. The he said: 'Hey, Micky....?'

'Yeah, Paddy.'

'What was wrong with blondie?'

'Wrong tickets.'

'Wrong tickets, oh yeah. Do you think we'll be late tonight, Micky?'

'Not sure, Paddy. Depends on the crowd.'

'Depends on the crowd. Oh yeah. Do you like this job, Micky?'

'It's ok, Paddy.'

'They're nice people, aren't they, Micky?'

'They're not too bad.'

'Ruby Walsh is riding later too, Micky.'

'Is he?'

'He is, Micky. Will you back him?'

'We're not supposed to back horses, Paddy.'

'Oh, yeah, oh yeah.'

A woman came along and said: 'I've no ticket but my kids don't know I smoke, so can I slip out there for a quick pull?'

I pulled back the door and she went outside.Braced the wind as she lit up, dragged hard and exhaled into the gratified cold. Paddy didn't say anything this time. We just sorta stood like sentries until something happened.

That's when mass started downstairs. The priest came over the speakers blessing the track, and the punters, and wishing everyone luck.

After, the commentator went through the line-up for the day. There was talk about Ruby Walsh but not much. I looked over and Paddy was gone somewhere. Probably to the jacks or for a sandwich or something. The woman came back from outside and said thanks, and she was rushing to put on a bet, and she ran off.

Few minutes later, the next race was on, and Paddy returned. You could hear him before you saw him. He shuffled when he walked, dragged his feet, and his jacket was too long and made a swoosh like an eagle's wings.

Jimmy the supervisor came too and he was holding a betting slip in his hand. I said: 'What's that?'

Got a good tip, he goes, from a steward. Ruby Walsh.

'Are we allowed to bet?'

He shrugged,said: 'Depends.' And walked off.

Later, when it was calm again, and the crowd were gone for a drink before the next race, it was just me and Paddy. I waited for him to open as I knew he would.

'Hey, Micky?'

'Yes, Paddy?'

'Did you back Ruby Walsh?'

'I didn't, Paddy, no. Did he win?'

'He did, came in at 22-1.

'Good man, Paddy.'

'You'd right to back him.'

'   'How much'd you win, Paddy?'

'I don't know. I have to collect it, yet. Do you think should I go and collect it, Micky?'

'You better, Paddy.'

'Do you think?'

'I do.'

'Will I go now?'

'Go on.'

'Right so, Micky. Thanks.'

'No problem, Paddy.'

'It's not a bad job when you make this kinda money, sure it isn't, Micky?'

Donedeal Dialogue

The phone rang and he opened with: 'How much d'ya want for the car, boss?'

'€650.'

'€650 you've up on the ad, but what'll you take for it?'

'What'll you give?'

'Ah, I don't know, sure is there no brakes on her?'

'No.'

'Or NCT?'

'Eh...no that's gone too.'

'And you want €650? Shtop, I'll give you €300.'

'I've already been offered €400 by a lad.'

'He must be on mushrooms?'

'That's what he offered.'

'Aragh, I don't know. How many miles on her?'

'355...thousand.'

Beat, then: 'Three hundred and fifty five THOUSAND?'

'Yeah, but she's a good car, never let me down....til now.'

'Ah, sham.'

'Wha?'

'Were you doin round trips to America in her?'

'No, just up and down the M6.'

'You want €650 for a car with no NCT, no brakes and three hundred and fifty five thousand miles on the clock?'

'I put two new tyres on her lately.'

'Sure what the fuck good are they with no brakes? Will she brake at all? Not even a little bit to get me home?'

'No. You'll need a truck or a tow rope to bring it.'

'There must be a little bitta *stop* in her...?'

'Nothin.'

'What's wrong them anyway?'

'Master Cylinder I think.'

'What's that?'

'I haven't a clue.'

'What about the handbrake?'

'That's broke too.'

'Are you serious?'

'I am.'

'Any tax?'

'Out next week.'

'Oh, Christ above. Sure, you're lookin for antique prices at this rate.'

'She's worth it.'

'You'll have to *pay* someone to take that away.'

'The engines are goin for export at €400

minimum.'

'Sure why would I want to export the engine? She'd be no good to me then at all.'

'I s'pose.'

'Hmm. Yeah. What's your best price so?'

'€450."

'Your *best price* I asked ya, c'mon on now. I'll give you €350 tonight, cash, into your paw, that's the besht you'll get.'

'I'll think about it.'

'No one else will give you that, and sure I'll probably hit the wall halfway up the road. Will you take €350 into the hand?'

'Depends on the other fella that offered €400.'

'Sure he's a pure fairy.'

'Money's *money.*'

'He won't give you that for it, you'll be wastin your time talkin to him. Take the cash off me now, quick sale. Into the pocket. Bang, she's done and dusted.'

'What time can you be here?'

'8 bells.'

'I'll call the other fella and if he's talkin shite I'll ring you back.'

'Do, do, do. I can be at your place tonight and we'll do a deal. That's the besht price you'll get.'

'G'luck.'

'Bye, ring me later so, bye so, bye.'

The Letter

Dark winter morning. Bedroom, stale oxygen. Clothes scattered on the floor, like half dead lazy dogs.

Monday.

The alarm rang for work. Jerome hit snooze again, a real proletarian hero.

Lorna's angry now. A sharp bite in the growing rage. 'Get up.'

'No.'

'Now! Come on, it's your own fault.'

'I hate Mondays.'

'That's coz you're always drunk on Sunday night.'

'I don't feel too good.'

'The kids'll be awake soon.'

'I think I'm going to get sick.'

'Out!'

He staggered to the bathroom. Looked at himself in the mirror, a mess of a man, a *nobody*, even by his own hungover standards. *Where's this all going?* He thought. *What's it all about, and why?* He took a box of painkillers from the cabinet. Swallowed two with soapy water from the tap then instantly fell to his knees and had a nuclear puke. It felt good, the pain of it, the torture.

Lorna, black nightdress, blonde hair, arms folded, listened to the heaving. Afterwards, he stumbled back under the covers, like a man back from the trenches after a dose of mustard gas.

'You stink of vomit.'

'I'm sorry.'

'Don't you ever feel like growing up?'

'Right now, I feel like never leaving this room.'

'Anything I should know about?'

He had a flashback of red hair, rouge painted nails, tears. It hit him like terror, a bad diagnosis. His pained eyes widened. 'Like what?'

'You know *like what*. Everyone behave themselves?'

'Of course.'

'*Everyone?*'

'Everyone.'

And he went to get sick again.

She got the kids up for school. Protests, arguments, clatter of breakfasts. A family scene, a loud scene, a snapshot of nostalgic noise for silent days to come.

Jerome called work, made up a story about one of the kids being sick, said he wouldn't be in. He hung up, got another flashback.

Black dress, tights, red shoes.

Did I...? Soon the children were gone and things got quiet enough to face the world. He came gingerly down the stairs, a soldier again, careful of mines, and just in time to see the post come through the letterbox. A singular speedy deposit from a delicate hand. Tender fingers through the slot. He stared down, it was addressed to him, sitting lonely on the floor. He picked it up and looked for a return address on the back, pulling a curious face as he'd been taught to do by so many countless films over the years.

There were seven words. He felt a melting dread, like blood rolling down the screen. The bad diagnosis again.

If you read this, you will die.

He stared at it for a couple of seconds, blinked, then read it once more. It was the same.

If you read this, you will die.

He walked into the kitchen. The world warping, a soft uncertain reality. Lorna said: 'What excuse did you give them this time?'

'Who?'

'Work, the place that pays the mortgage.'

She looked over. His worried expression: 'What's wrong?'

He held it up, said: 'I don't know.'

'Let me see that.'

Except for the address, it was completely white.

She examined it closely and said: 'Weird. What is it?'

'How should I know?'

'Will I open it?'

'Should you?'

'Well it says *you* will die, so I should be ok.'

'What if it's like, some really bad news?'

'Like what? It's just a prank or whatever. You can't die from opening a letter.'

'What about letter-bombs? Or anthrax?'

'And they just thought they'd mention it on the back?'

She took a scissors from the kitchen drawer. No searching, swift, a weapon made for the moment. The blade went swiftly through the enemy and a folded piece of paper fell out. They exchanged glances. He thought of the first time he'd seen her, that night in the club. *Did I ever love her at all?*

'Well?' Said Lorna.

He snaps back, says: 'Just throw it in the fire.'

'Now? No way. I want to read it.'

'Be careful.'

Sunshine came through the window behind her as she read. A Victorian scene, a woman of letters, news from the front. There was a lingering smell of toast. She squinted at the words. Jerome was getting impatient, anxious. He should have just binned it. He could see the writing was very neat. Not a long letter, but a decent amount of words. Two paragraphs maybe. That auntie in America? She's into writing, but not this weirdness.

He watched Lorna for a reaction, waited for a relieved laugh, a comedic explanation. Her eyes grew wide as if she was trying to digest something combustible. His hangover blazed again, a raging wildfire, enjoying new life. He looked at the sink as an emergency option. Cold dinosaur sweat ran across his back now and down his legs. His stomach lashed with scaly green peptic lava. She put it down with a snap and said: 'You bastard.'

'Huh?'

'You bastard, how dare you? Who do you think you are?'

'What does it say?'

'You know *exactly* what it says. You're a liar and a bastard.'

'Hang on a second, Lorna, what's it say? Am I going to die? Just relax, and show it to me.'

'Get out.'

'Listen, I don't know...'

She picked up the frying pan. 'I'm giving you thirty seconds to leave.'

'But...'

He ducked as the pan clamoured off the wall behind him. It went kwang, clunk, gronk and fell into the sink and smashed three plates. Lorna threw a cup next. Tea lacerated the wall, left a long-tailed stain, like it came from a meteor that was really a tea bag.

He ran into the hallway, grabbed his jacket, a haunted man, running from evil. He opened the front door. Morning air, embraced him, like an invisible school of affectionate fish. He looked back, she was raging towards him with a sweeping brush, demonic eyes, a scene from a zombie film.

He tripped on the step and landed on the path outside. She gave him a skelp with the brush, then stood at the door and screamed: 'And take your fucking letter with you!'

He was flat on his back, looking at the sky, as he heard the door slam. The letter swirled and landed at his feet. He was tempted to read it but was too afraid now. The drink, nerves, the fear. It was all too much. He stood up slowly, groaned at the effort, shoved the letter in his pocket, and tried to avoid the looks of the neighbours through their twitching curtains.

Blue eyes, perfect teeth, cream skin of impossible youth. Her black underwear. What did I do...?

He shuddered, walked towards the town.

He needed a strong drink.

Fast.

Broke, and still in his night clothes, *Rabbitte's* was his only option. He was a good friend of the owner, Paddy. He'd have a few there and wait for it all to blow over. He had a craving for a smooth cider and a few small ones to take the edge off.

Inside the bar. It was busy. A healthy economy of drinkers. No seats at the counter. All the lads in from the night before, like pigs at the trough, swallowing down pints. They cheered when they saw him, but then fell into silent, frightened concern. Blood on his face, the slippers, what the fuck? Finally, from behind the bar, Paddy spoke. flannel shirt, towel, not bald yet. 'Alright Jerome, everything ok?'

Jerome didn't know what to say. Paddy continued: 'Want to come round the back for a chat?'

Jerome did. Walked through. Into the empty lounge. It was dark, dusty, and smelled like an old couch. A pool table sat bored in the middle and a dartboard hung idle on the wall. The only light came from a flashing arcade game in the corner. *Space Invaders*, maybe *Pong*? He couldn't remember.

Paddy smelled like apricot, asked: 'What the hell happened to you?'

He put his head in his hands, said: 'I don't know, Paddy. The whole fuckin world's gone belly up.'

The other men watched from the front as Paddy filled a double whisky like a medic in the tent, the man with the painkillers. He came back and said: 'Drink that, it'll settle ya. Did ya get robbed or kicked or what?'

He floored the whisky, winced, and Paddy refilled it. 'I was at home with the wife, you know?'

Paddy nodded. Barman nod, a real king of the nods.

'Yeah, yeah. Go on.'

'Next thing we get the post...'

He drained the glass again, felt it go straight to his veins, like chariots of courage.

'Go on, ya got the post, yeah, go on…'

He left the letter on the counter. 'And this came for me.'

Paddy picked it up, frowned like a man that knew how to frown, asked: 'What you do? Get some young wan pregnant? I told ya to be careful with that Murphy one.'

'Read the back of it.'

Paddy flipped it over, said: 'Jesus. What's it say inside?'

'How do you mean?'

'Well, did you read it?'

'No.'

'No?'

'No! Well would *you*?'

'Yeah, no, I dunno.'

'Lorna read it. Went mental. Tried to kill me with a frying pan.'

'But *why*? What could be *that* bad?'

'That's what I'm afraid to know.'

Paddy took a towel from his shoulder and wiped the counter.

'Strangest thing I heard now in a long time…think she'll snap out of it?'

'Fuckin hope so.'

'Tell ya what, go upstairs and get yourself cleaned up. I'll get ya some clothes and that. You can have a few pints on me. Get me later. I'll say nothing to the lads. Everythin'll be sound again by the evening.'

'Ah, I don't know Paddy, that's an awful lot

of hassle.'

'Go on. You're alright.'

Jerome thought. Out of options, he said: 'Ok, I'll hit the jacks and work it from there. Thanks, Paddy.'

'You're alright, go on.'

In the toilet. Bright white walls and smell of piss and detergent. Two cubicles, one with the door hanging off, like it had been kicked. He splashed his face with water, thought: *You're some taypot, Jerome.* Rubbed his eyes, rough skin, stubble through his fingers. A guilty scene, a man on the run, unsure, hunted. He was weak with vague fear and a shaky prelude to panic. Loud noises scared him. That water from the tap, roaring like Niagara Falls. All things are triggers, hypersonic bells on his weak nerves. He'd need another few shots to settle down, get some perspective. That nausea coming on again. Would need to bury it in more alcoholic concrete.

On the plus side, he felt safe with Paddy, a friend he could trust. And maybe it *was* all a joke. Or maybe it *was* Karen Murphy? He'd broken it off a month ago and she hadn't taken it well. Sure she was still in school, the fuckin babysitter. Threatened him with telling Lorna. But this? What's next, boil his dog in the kitchen saucepan? Christ, he'd give her some bollocking when he saw her.

He walked out, smothered the thought, let the day crush the past, like a tin can in a compactor, but his mood lost altitude when he saw Paddy leaning over the front counter, with the letter in his hand, pointing at certain words. The lads at the bar, huddled together, squinted at the sentences. Men that rarely read, but looked for the signal in the noise, the dominant emotion. In this case it would be *violence.*

When they saw Jerome they all played the statue, concerned mimes, holding pints. Paddy whispered something and walked over. They all watched him for guidance.

'Well?'

'Well what, Jerome? What's this about, eh? Who the hell do you think you are? Sure no wonder she threw you out.'

No more friendly talk of free drink.

'Look, Paddy, I don't know what's in the damn letter, but I swear to god, whatever it is, there was no harm intended to anyone.'

'Harm! Huh? That's one for the books.'

Octaves getting higher now. The other men ansty, feeling their way through the decibels, noise inspired amoebas, the shrieking atoms like banshees, dying to assemble and cause havoc.

'Tell ya what, Jerome, piss off. I don't want you in here anymore. You're bad for business. Get out.'

'What the hell're you talking about?'

'You know well what I'm talking about. Seriously, what're ya at? Coming in here dressed like that, looking for sympathy, then coming up with *this*?'

'I don't know what it says. But if that's Murphy one, I swear ta God...'

'Sure, it's nothin to do with the Murphy girl. She's a saint compared to a prick like you.'

'She didn't send it?'

Paddy looked at the letter again, went for ultra-sarcastic with: 'Don't you wish your problems were that fuckin small....'

One of the men at the front counter shouted over. 'If Paddy said you should leave, then we think you should leave.'

He was backed by the crowd in the stern movements and mutters.

'What?'

'We read it too. We don't want you in here anymore.'

'Read what? This?' He picked it up. 'It's just a letter, how *bad* can it be? You're all such a pack of lunatics, it's me, *Jerome.* You know me.'

'We thought we did,' said another lad, halfway through a lager, drinking up the mob vehemence.

'Look, Jerome,' said Paddy, 'just go while you still can.'

The pool table creaked, hear the low din of country music from the crackling radio. Chasms debated; oracles whined. Jerome decided to go Clint Eastwood and hope it work out. Long shot we know, but it was that kind of day.

He folded his arms, said: 'No way, not until

we sort out this mess. Only five minutes ago Paddy was standing me drink for the day. Forget it, I'm staying here.'

Paddy turned to the other customers, said: 'Might need a hand here, lads.'

Pseudo Clint finds himself on the ground, trying to protect his head from a torrent of kicks. Not the type of script he had conjured up twenty seconds ago but here we are. Each blow produced a white, painful flash. From behind, he guessed it was Paddy, a pair of hands came under his shoulders and dragged him away. The shower of violence continued to the door. He saw everything in snaps and objects. A boot. A ceiling. An angry face. White stars. The passing tables. The street outside. Paddy standing over him.

'And take your dirty letter with ya.'

-

He woke up by the river. The cops standing over him, responding to a call about a disturbance. Someone had reported a homeless man stealing Jack Daniels from the supermarket. They watched him now, shaking their heads. One of them was a woman. Sharp, bitter, strict. The other a man. Long term, resigned to having seen it all. Jerome tried to talk but his mouth was numb. They asked him where he lived and he could only mumble. The drink, the swollen mouth, and some missing teeth. It was all garbage. He struggled to stand up, couldn't make it off the ground, and kept making bizarre shapes and signals with his hands. The guards exchanged a concerned look.

'What d'ya think?' Asked the man.

'Bring him in, I suppose. Might be better able to talk when he sobers up a bit.'

'Wonder who he is?'

'Probably one of the junkies. They're gone to hell around the place lately.'

She picked up the bottle, said: 'Definitely him we got the call about anyway.'

They lifted his legs and she noticed something on the ground.

'Look at this.'

'What's that?'

'Some kind of a letter left here beside him.'

'Bring it with ya, might be an address or something. Let's get him into the car for now.'

-

Jerome woke with a wonderful pain in his head. Nagasaki flashes, neurons burning on the tortured face of Saturn.

He sat up and looked around. He was in a cell. White cold walls. Footsteps on the corridor outside, and the rattling of keys. Something made a loud knocking noise. He looked up. It was a big burly man with thin legs, hitting his baton off the steel bars. His red curls were barely visible under the blue cap.

'Wakey, wakey.'He said, through the squeezed air of the obese.

'Where am I?'

'The station.'

'What happened? How did I get here?'

'You were drunk and disorderly, making a nuisance of yourself on the street, couldn't even talk. Are you from the wake?'

'What wake?'

'The big one.'

He stuttered. 'No... no wake...just a letter.'

'A letter?'

'Yes.'

'What kind of a letter?'

'I don't know, I haven't read it.'

The guard stood staring. We'll call him Tommy, fuck it. He tapped his baton some more. 'Think you're still a bit steamed. Don't suppose you know where you live?'

'Forster Court.'

'Forster Court?'

'Yes. 102.'

'But that's a respectable place.'

'I know.'

'Get some more sleep and we'll talk in a while.'

Tommy walked away, jangling his keys and whistling.

Later, a voice said: 'You're awake?'

Jerome looked up, saw it was the guard that arrested him. Grey eyes like mountain rain. Puzzled by the question, Jerome replied: 'Yes.'

'Good.'

'Why's that?'

'We have to talk to ya.'

'About what?'

'Getting ya home.'

'Thank god for that.'

'What's your name?'

'Jerome.'

'I'm John. Get up and follow me.'

'Where to?'

'You'll have to pay the shop for the drink you stole. Then home. Forster Court, is it?'

'Yeah.'

They walked up through a long corridor. More guards. Some doing paperwork, others on the phone. A peaceful scene, oil on canvas, cop station. Jerome was feeling relief, surrounded by pillars of sense, back on sure ground, terrain he recognized.

But then.

'Hey, sarge,' called John. 'Just droppin this fella back to Forster Court. Need anything in town?'

'No, you're alright.'

They were almost out when the sergeant asked: 'By the way, John, do you know anything about this letter? Found it over there on the desk.'

John looked, said: 'Ah yeah got it on this boyo here.' He pointed at Jerome and continued with: 'Picked him up by the river this morning.'

The sergeant got cloudy, ominous, looked at Jerome, said: 'Oh yeah? Have you read it?'

'No, not yet. Why?'

Conspiratorial now. 'Come back here to the office for a second.'

Through the glass door, Jerome watched, fairly sure where this was all going.

John looked confused as he held it in his hand. The sergeant pointing at certain words.

The other officers were all attention, watching Jerome, waiting for him to run.

Naturally he ran.

But they were on him like a falling church.

Twenty seconds later he was handcuffed and badly bruised. The men returned from the office with grim faces. John asked: 'Tried to escape, eh? Well, no need to worry about that now, we have a nice little plan for ya. Soon you'll be getting all the holidays you need.'

The sergeant came over and said: 'What a fuckin mess.'

Jerome, with filthy feet and torn, bloodstained pyjamas, could barely disagree.

'You write this?'

He squinted, with blackened eyes, glops of blood on his teeth.

'Eh?' The sergeant continued. 'It's scum like you that make our job hell. Freaks like you that give the country a bad name. If it was up to me, you'd all be shot. Who the hell do you think you are? Comin in here with letters like this?'

He punched Jerome on the jaw. It made a tearing crack, like walking on bubble wrap. Jerome wondered how he'd explain that to the dentist, and how much it would cost, and then the pain set in and he thought he'd pass out.

'Fucking scumbag, get him out of here.' He turned to John and said: 'You know what to do.'

It was half an hour's drive to the shipyard. Scenic, narrow road, drizzle. John didn't make much talk. Playing the grumpy game. Two hands on the wheel, fixated on the journey. Jerome felt hot, a flashback to childhood, his father, in that old car, smoking a cigarette through the country music. But no such music here, just radio static and a crackled voice saying *let us know when you've that bollocks got rid of...*

The car pulled into the yard, angry on the gravel, portentous proximity to the sea. There was a man carrying boxes into the stomach of a big boat, like he was feeding it cargo. He looked like a *Brendan*. Tea cosy hat, black thick jacket, brown boots.

He turned round, glanced at his watch, frowned, said: 'John?'

John was out, all business, affirmative tone and stance, impressing the authority and gravity of the uniform. 'Slight emergency.' He said.

'What ya got?'

'Troublemaker.'

Brendan walked over to the back of the car, opened the door, looked at Jerome, like a farmer assessing a sick animal. 'Not too small, but we'll fit him in somewhere. Why the panic?

'You're on a *need-to-know* basis.'

'Usual fee?'

John produced a brown envelope, said: 'A bit extra for the short notice.'

Sound, said Brendan, let me go and make a bit of space.

Brendan left. John turned, caught Jerome by the collar, sack of spuds job, and pulled him from the back of the car and hissed: 'Now, Jerome, listen carefully, you're not wanted here. Nobody wants you in this town anymore. Puttin you on this ship is a favour. Do the wise thing and *don't* come back. We won't be so nice to you the next time, d'ya hear me?'

*

Later, he was in a small cabin, tiny round window, a smell like bleach and burnt carpet. He felt seasick. Poisoned.

Brendan pushed open the door.

Jerome asked: 'What am I doing here?'

When Brendan spoke, it reverberated around the room. 'Headed for America. How's all them aches and pains? You were in a right mess.'

'America!'

'Relax, son. Don't get too excited, someone might hear ya, and you not supposed to be here at all. You'll get us both in bother.'

'America!'

'Shss...' He took out a small syringe. 'This will help you sleep and you'll be able to think better when ya wake.'

'Hang on.'

But it was too late. Everything went blank, black, blacker and sank into nothing and nowhere. The next day. Sun off the ocean, spraying like rays from a cracked mirror. Brendan stood over him with the syringe, asked Jerome if he was going to be quiet. He said he would, but needed an explanation.

Brendan sighed, said:'You're goin to America.'

'But why?'

'Coz you weren't wanted at home, that's what John does.'

'How do you mean?'

'Well, there's no point in havin you hanging around in jail or walking the streets while you're waitin for a trial. Folks don't like it, so he sends ya to me and I plant ye in the states until things blow over.'

'Yeah but... I'm not a criminal.'

'John says you are.'

'He's wrong.'

'He's never wrong.'

'This time he is.'

'Then why did he send you here?'

Jerome was silent. The letter roared in his shirt pocket, like tormented demons trapped between the folds of the delicate paper.

'Thing is, lad, you weren't wanted. He did the right thing. If you stayed, it would have been a lot worse for you and for everyone else. This way,

I get a few pound and you get a long holiday. The sooner you accept that the better.'

'I want to go home.'

'Of course you do. But whatever type of trouble you're in has to settle. There's no point goin home when people are out to get ya.'

Jerome felt logic dawn in the fug of his mind. And he wasn't going to let it go. Logic was an endangered species. Practically extinct. Brendan continued: 'I'll give you a uniform and you can work on the deck with me until we get there. Nobody will notice. After we get to New York, you're on your own.'

He left and Jerome sat thinking on the bed. He felt for the letter. Took it out. Looked at it. Should he read it? No, not yet. Not here, on a boat, in the middle of the ocean. Who knows what might happen if...if what? What was he afraid of?

He blinked, wondered, *what the hell is after happening*?

And fell asleep again.

*

He woke up on the wet deck. Smell of sea air. He thought of mussels, crabs, prawns, oysters. His hands and legs were tied. He could barely move.

'Who the hell do you think you are?' Said Brendan, as he dragged him along. 'This is the worst I've ever seen. Absolute evil. And me taking pity on a bollocks like you. A man tries to take care of you and look what he finds?'

Fuck.

'Hang on, Brendan, just hang on.'

'I'll not hang on. No, I bloody won't.'

Gulls flew overhead. Wide wings blocking out the sun.

Brendan untied a lifeboat. Picked up Jerome, like a sack of rice, and threw him inside. Jerome saw stars, got a swift dose of vertigo, then radiating pain down his entire back.

Brendan said: 'I'll be having a word with John after this.'

'Let's just talk for a second.' Groaned Jerome.

'I have standards about who I transport.'

It hurt to talk, think, breathe. 'I'm ok, Brendan. I'm not what you think I am.'

Brendan hooked the lifeboat to a pulley. 'It's too late for explanations.'

'What are you doin?'

'Gettin rid of vermin like you...'

Brendan stuffed the letter into Jerome's top pocket and then let the rope fall rapidly through the pulley. Breeze went by like passing prayers that Jerome couldn't catch.

Down down down, his stomach gulped, his bones tensed, he clenched his teeth against the crash. And crash it did. Landed on the ocean with force, anger, and a dramatic splash. The sea gushed in around his feet, into his eyes and mouth, hungry as a starved dog. He tasted salt and something like petrol. Brendan was shouting but he couldn't hear it because the ship was already pulling away.

-

What now, taypot? If I'm going to die, says he, then I've nothing to lose from reading the letter. And good thing the fall broke the rope that had his hands tied. He took it out of his top pocket. It was still folded but he could see the famous sentences. He fumbled for a second and almost lost it in the wind.

The words danced between the corners, giving him a teasing glimpse, but not enough to read. His neck protested from the stress, and the breeze got stronger, rearing up. Eventually he got it open, managed a confident grip, and got his head at the proper angle to see the

Meeting The Sniper

The night came, over the hills as the orb dropped, a ball of red life, retreating, like a dying dream. We got to Lawrence, Kansas, in a slow shuffled stop of squealing brakes. Arrived at a deserted station under the lonely full moon, where you might hallucinate a solitary man in a long coat, standing quietly on the platform, under the mysterious lunar mist. And the trees were still and patient, ancient and calm. And people smoked like minor cancers in the serene ecosystem, chlorophyllic infections from the loud combusting carriages. And a guy asked me for a light and I told him I had none and he got one off the ticket guy and then we got talking. He was tall. Blonde. Baby-faced. Agile. Where ya goin, what ya doin, where ya from, nice train, quiet night.

'I'm Mick.'

'I'm Mike, it's really Mikhail cos I have Russian origins.'

'I'm really Michéal cos it's Irish for Michael.'

'Cool. Going to Vegas, huh?'

'Yeah. You?'

'I gotta report for duty in the morning.'

'Duty?'

'I'm in The Marines.'

'Full Metal Jacket job?'

'Kind of. I got a five-man squadron and we're getting deployed next week.'

'Iraq?

'Afghanistan.'

'I heard it's getting messy over there.'

He took a long drag, smoke in the night, hovers in the lamplight, stars playing notes like the music of astronomy.

Mikhail said: 'It was never any other way, man.'

'Will you have to kill anyone?'

'I got my crew and we watch out for the guys on the ground.'

'Making sure they know what they're getting into?'

'Yeah, I'm a sniper.'

There was a judder in the timeline, like that moment the car loses power, just for a second, and then you're back.

He continued: 'We *protect*.'

'Are ya long doin it?'

'Couple of years. I was recruited because I can speak Russian and I'm trained in multiple marital arts.'

The whistle goes and we get back inside. He went one way. I went the other. The windows were black with night. I took a seat (bright ocean blue) and drank red wine and thought about Vegas and war. The Amish guy opposite me looked over occasionally and smiled. Him and his red cheeks and his side-burns. And the train beat rhythms on the quiet tracks, like wheels on an office chair going over a plush carpet. We stopped again, a slow descent into another American town. People woke, searched for suitcases, left through the dark unknowable doors.

Mikhail came back out for another smoke and we picked up where we left off.

'When we're in action, we're trained to never move. Go to the toilet. Nothing. We have to sit still for hours. Even days.'

'Why?'

'You can't give your position away. Even the slightest move and you're gone.'

'How long you goin out there for?'

'Depends. Some tours are six months. Others twelve and eighteen.'

'And you have a choice?'

'I don't care. I'm staying out there as long as I can. I want to protect my country, man. Someone needs to. And if I don't, those motherfuckers are gonna come and shoot me, and my family, and whoever else they can kill.'

'What are the civilian casualties like?'

'I'll put it like this. The other week, right, a good friend of mine, good guy, fuckin good soldier. He's out there, and he's doing his job, and he's trying to help the villagers fight these Taliban assholes, cos those guys are bad, right?'

'Right.'

'So a young girl, about eight, comes up to him saying: '...hey mister, hey mister...' Something like that. And she's sweet and she's holding a doll and he wants to be kind cos she's a kid and these are things she's gonna remember when she gets older, right? Hearts and minds.'

'Hearts and minds.'

'So she hands him the doll and he takes it and the fuckin thing explodes and kills the two of them.'

He smokes more, says: 'Crazy, right? So that's what we're up against. Some of those guys don't care, at least *we* have standards. I love my country. I'll die to protect it, but I won't kill a child in the process. That's the difference between us and them. That's what people don't understand.'

'What age are you, Mikhail?'

Stubs out his cigarette. 'I'm just gone twenty-five.'

'Twenty-five.'

'Yeah, it's hard on my girlfriend, but she said she'll wait. Whatever it takes. Ya know?'

Time to get back on board. The Amish guy was gone. I had most of the carriage to myself. Rain fell light on the window, massaged the glass, a casual collection of disinterested drops, witness to the secrets of the American wind as she whispers across the empty plains.

Later, the train docked in reverence at Kingston and sat with a disengaged silence as we got off into the dusty desert night. That woman with the walking aid. The Chinese man with the white headphones. Outside, everything was orange lamplight and hot tar and wonder, and amplified sounds like the clicking of backpacks and suitcase wheels on concrete. I saw Mikhail there with his bags packed, ready to go, walking up the road, like a nonchalant hitchhiker. He looked around, spotted me and said: 'Hey, Mick, good luck in Vegas.'

And he was gone.

The Living Room

Writing during working hours every day is great in theory. Start at nine. Finish at five. Simple. Until you're stone broke and pure sick from drink. Some evenings you go out for one pint and end up rollerblading the prom at four in the morning, trying to keep your balance, with a can in one hand and a naggin in the other, and you never having rollerbladed before in your life.

You get up the next morning and you look at your computer and you know there isn't a hope of making sense. That's if you came home at all. Often you'd end up back at a house party of some crowd you're only after meeting and you wake up on the floor not knowing who the hell they are. Your teeth feel like they're wrapped in cotton wool and your tongue is welded to the roof of your mouth, and that dodgy kebab is doing ya no good at all.

And an odd night you might go home to your own place, and that's not too bad, except for the strays you picked up along the way.

You go down to the sitting room to get the laptop and there's two or three bodies thrown on the floor, surrounded by empty cans and dead phones. And the garlic smell of perspired drink would knock a horse.

And you know your housemates aren't happy because it was a Tuesday night and this sort of thing isn't acceptable to *working people.* They were woke up at three by Paddy pressing the doorbell and again at four by Laura looking for the toilet and walking into their bedroom. At five, James got in a fight with Tom about Northern Ireland and broke a bottle off the wall. Now there's glass all over the floor and James and Tom are nowhere to be seen. When Laura came back from the toilet, she wanted toast and raided all the presses until she found rashers and eggs and tried to cook them all. She burnt the rashers and set the smoke alarm off and got such a fright she spilled the saucepan of boiling eggs all over the floor. She eventually went to the 24-hour shop and bought a jambon and a bar of chocolate and, when she got back, kept pressing the doorbell to get back in.

Then Paddy, full of Dutch Gold and courage, tried his case with Laura but she has a fella. They'd had a fight earlier and he's been ringing her all night but she won't answer and she won't put the phone on silent either. Eventually her and Paddy fall asleep on the ground in a spooning position and it's just you and Gary drinking fifty cent lagers from Lidl and talking shite about American politics and conspiracy theories around 9/11, and JFK, and Roswell and the Moon Landing.

So now it's the morning and your head feels like it's full of an expanding glacier of pain. You make a fuzzy attempt to clean up while the others sit around and watch. Laura's trying to book a taxi but she doesn't know the address. Paddy's wondering where's a good place to get a full Irish breakfast. Gary's rolling a cigarette on the couch and says the *Living Room* is a great spot for food. And they do lovely Heineken. So we all go there and you promise to write twice as much tomorrow. To make up for today's lost word count. And the housemates need time to calm down. It'll all get sorted. Just need to eat first. And get some of that Heineken to take the edge off. And it's Wednesday. And it's not even noon.

Requiem For A Field

John felt it all slipping away. The big blow, the moment when it would all make sense. There was a hole he couldn't fill, a punctured darkness somewhere in his soul, and the air was escaping, slow but permanent. And there was a poker game on in the local pub.

He turned to Mary and said: 'I need your blessing.'

'I won't give it to you. You'll lose, like you always did before. Like everyone does when they gamble.'

'It's just bad luck, Mary. I'll come back with enough to buy us a trailer load of cattle, and maybe a weekend away somewhere.'

'If you go out that door, you'll ruin us.'

'You won't be saying that tomorrow.'

'If I'll be here at all. We're in enough debt as it is without your notions.'

'It's an innocent bit of fun.'

She turned up the volume on the television. Her passive-aggressive way of ending the argument. John lingered, for the record, giving her a chance to believe in him, then pulled the door back in mock rage and stormed out.

Outside, it began to rain. He buttoned up his thick black coat. His feet rustled through the dead leaves and the dark puddles. There was a leak in his shoe and he felt the damp seep through the sock on his right foot. The game was on in *Quinn's,* the busiest pub in the village. The owner, Rory, was always trying something different. He had done everything from karaoke competitions to bingo, and now poker. It wasn't a popular choice at first but lately it was gathering interest. Many of the local elite regarded it as a new thrill. They wanted to flash their wealth, and *poker* seemed the perfect way to do it.

The entry fee was €250. John had taken the money from a savings jar. Mary had walked in and caught him and that's where the argument began. He put his hand in his pocket now and rubbed the notes between his fingers.

She's wrong, he said to himself. *Everyone is wrong. I'll show them all.*

He passed the Mahon's place on the right. Everybody knew that family. They'd come up from the city and built a fine row of mansions just outside the village. At first, everyone welcomed the business. The local plasterers, electricians, and block layers were all hired on a contract basis. It was agreed that each tradesman would see to the five houses and then get paid in full at the end. Suspecting little, the work was done, and the men awaited their wages, but were never paid. They brought a joint case to a local solicitor and a legal demand for payment was sent. Days later, each of the men received an unexpected visit. Although the reasons were never discussed, the case was dropped immediately and nothing more was said about the money.

The pub was already busy. A line of men stood at the bar and the distinctive click of casino chips could be heard in the background. The pool table had been pushed aside to make space and all the tables were covered in green felt like you would see in Las Vegas. A double Jameson later, John felt confident enough to go around and talk to some of the other customers. They were all there for the game, watching the clock, anxiously awaiting the call to be seated.

He handed over the money and received his stack. They were blue, white, red, and reminded him of the *Connect 4* game he'd had as a child.

Suddenly there was a hush as somebody entered. People stood up, craned their necks over tall shoulders and squinted to see what the fuss was about. Pakie Mahon stood by the entrance. He was the most feared of the family and was reputed to have links with the deadliest of the city gangs. As the silence continued he said: 'Is it a ghost ye're all after seeing, or what?'

Everyone mumbled and went back to their drinks. Pakie went to the counter and bought his poker chips. He was dressed in a black Nike trouser tracksuit, a white Umbro jacket and bright, white runners. He wore an earring in both ears and was chewing gum. Teddy O'Neil, a timid man from the next village, seeing that Pakie would be playing, stood up and asked for a refund.

The game started. A few people quietly asked Rory to throw Pakie out but he was reluctant to listen as the place might get burned down as a result.

John had a good run and played his cards well. He came close to elimination but luck was on his side and the others, intimidated by Pakie, didn't last too long.

Soon, there was only two players left.

John and Pakie Mahon.

The estimated pot was €10000.

John was feeling confident. He'd had a few more double Jameson and was resolved to playing an aggressive game. All the other players were gathered round to see the final battle.

'What's it gonna be, Burkie?' Asked Pakie.

'How d'ya mean?'

'Well, I'm goin to clean ya. How do you feel about that? We can split the pot now if ya like and save ya the bruisin....'

'We'll play for it,' said John.

'But you'll get nothin goin that way.'

'We'll see.'

The cards were dealt. John got a three and a six. Pakie raised the bet immediately, putting pressure on him from the start. John pretended to think about it, and eventually folded.

'Had nothin, eh? Me neither.' Said Pakie.

John tried to neuter his impatience, but soon began to make irrational bets and stupid decisions. He was desperate to win but began to feel uncertain, like he wasn't anchored to the situation.

'Not goin your way, Burkie.' Said Pakie, as he took a long draught of Guinness.

John finished another whisky and said: 'Shut up and play.'

'That's a good sports man for ya, boy.'

The dealer said: 'Your turn, Mr. Mahon.'

John had a pair of queens. He hoped this was his chance.

Suddenly Pakie said: 'Raise.'

John's legs went weak. It took all his energy to stay composed. He acted stressed, counted his chips, and said: 'Call.'

The crowd drew closer and everything went eerily quiet. They wanted to see Pakie *lose*. To see him humiliated. If John won this hand, he would take him out completely.

The first three cards came out. A queen, an ace and a six. John could hardly restrain himself.

'Raise.' Said Pakie.

'Call.'

The fourth card was turned. A two.

After inspecting his cards, Pakie said: 'All in.'

John felt doubt. He looked at all the possibilities. He thought Pakie might have a pair of aces, or maybe he might get a full house. But it was a risk he was prepared to take. If he didn't make his big move now, he'd be too far behind to pose a serious threat and almost certainly lose. He made the only decision he could and said: 'Call.'

'On their backs.' Said the dealer.

John flipped his pair of queens and Pakie's face dropped. He only had a pair of sixes. John looked down to see that only another six could beat him. He was already anticipating the look on Mary's face when he came home with the €10000.

'Ah, Burkie. What are ya doin to me?'

'That's poker.'

'She's not over yet, boy.'

The dealer turned the river card. A five. Everyone clapped, less out of joy for John than at the loss for Pakie.

John told Rory to fill a drink for the house. Everyone was talking excitedly about the drama. Nobody noticed as Pakie reached into his pocket for a new stick of chewing gum, switching the deck of cards at the same time. When the noise died down, he said: 'That was good, Burkie. You're not bad.'

'Thanks, Pakie. Can I buy you a drink?'

'No. But we can have a private game, if ya like? Just the two of us.'

'What stakes?' Asked John, tempted.

'Cash game.'

'No, maybe some other time, thanks.'

'Why not? At least give me a chance to win

my stake back, like.'

'I won't play for cash. It's too...'

'Is Burkie afraid?'

John blushed as some bystanders tuned in. 'No, I just want to...'

'Are ye playin again?' Asked someone from the crowd.

'They're playin again.' Said someone else.

'Cash game!' Said a third.

Before John knew it, he was sitting face to face with Pakie Mahon and the €10000 was up for grabs again.

Within two hours, Pakie was smiling as John sweated. A lot of people had gone home. Only a few quiet drinkers and Rory Quinn, yawning behind the bar, remained. John counted his money. He had €1500 left. He could walk away with €1250 profit or...

Pakie raised the bet and waited for his reaction. John looked at his cards, left them down, and forgot what they were. There was a metallic taste in his mouth and his eyes felt heavy as blocks. For the first time he realized he was drunk.

'All of them in...' He slurred, trying to sound confident, as he pushed his final chips towards the centre.

Pakie called immediately. He sounded so sure that John knew he had already lost. As the cards were turned, he put his head on the table and felt like crying. Pakie reached over and scooped up the last of the money and said: 'Hard luck, Burkie boy. Hard luck.'

John looked up and said: 'That's my money. You cheated, you dirty gangster. Give it back to me.'

Pakie's tone changed. 'Watch your mouth now, Burkie. A game's a game.'

'Shag off back to the city, ya thug.'

Rory Quinn stepped in, said: 'That's enough, John. I'll drive you home.'

John slurred. 'I want a chance to win my money back.'

Rory said: 'C'mon now, John. Leave it at that.'

'No. One more hand.'

'With *what*?' Asked Pakie.

'You have nothin left.' Said Rory.

'I have land.' said John. '500 acres of it.'

Pakie perked up and said: 'If the man wants to...'

'No!' Said Rory. 'Game over. My place. My rules.'

'I want to play.' Drawled John.

'One hand.' Said Pakie. 'You win, I'll give you the €10000 back. I win, you give me that fine field you have. The one behind my uncle Joe's house down by the main road.'

John looked up, said: 'How do you know what fields I have?'

'I'm in the development business, Burkie. It's my job to know.'

Rory caught John under the arms, said:

'C'mon.'

'No!' Said John, pushing Rory away. 'I'll play him. He thinks he knows it all, but I'll show him.'

'Let the man play, Mr. Quinn. He's an adult, like myself and yourself.'

'He's drunk is what he is. It's not right...'

'None of your business, Mr. Quinn. You don't want to be getting on anybody's bad side now, d'ya hear? Here's €500 for yourself and we'll let things take their course now, what do you reckon?"

Rory eyed the money, looked at John, back at the cash and said: 'Alright, go on. But half an hour and I'm closing up and that's it.'

The dealer put up his palms, said: 'I'm having no part of this. Do what ye like. I'm off home. It's too late for this messing.' He picked up his jacket and left.

Pakie winked, said: 'Just me and you so, Burkie. I suppose I'll have to deal.'

John's eyes watered. He found it hard to concentrate and a sense of desperation was all he could comprehend. He didn't consider the loss of the field. He didn't even imagine it was going to happen. All he wanted was the €10000 back. It was close enough to touch, but he just needed one good hand.

'You understand now, Burkie, that a deal's a deal. If you wake up in the mornin and decide you don't want to part with that field, a few of the lads will be over to change your mind. You know what

I'm sayin to ya?'

      'That won't happen.'

      'You're sure now, Burkie?'

      'Deal the cards.'

The Phone Call

Rachel asked: 'Can I use your phone?'

'Why?'

'I need to ring an 1800 number and I have no credit.'

'Ok.'

I gave it to her. She dialled. There was phone music. Then a myriad of options. She chose one. Then it went through to customer service and a woman answered with: 'What's your account number, please?'

She cleared her throat, said: 'Joe rang ye half an hour ago.'

'Excuse me?'

'Do you remember Joe rang ye? About half an hour ago?'

'I'm sorry, I don't understand.'

'I need ye to send me a letter.'

'Eh...let me see. Do you have an account with us?'

'Not yet.'

'And you'd like to set one up?'

'Joe is doing it for me. He rang ye half an hour ago. But my phone has no credit now, see. I'm usin this fella's phone here beside me and I just want to see what ye said to Joe.'

'I'm sorry, but I don't think it was me he was talking to.'

'Who was he talking to, so?'

'I have no idea.'

'But he rang ye.'

'I know, you mentioned that. Can you explain why he rang?'

'To get me set up.'

'Ok, I can do that for you now if you like?'

'You need to send me the letter first.'

'What letter?'

'To say I don't owe ye anythin.'

'Ok. And do you owe us anything?'

'No. See. I did in the last place, but I paid it off, but now I'm in a new place and I need ye to send me the letter to say I'm clear with ye.'

'I see. That should be simple. What was your account number in the last place?'

'I don't have it. See Joe has all the details.'

'Ok, let me see. What's your phone number?'

'I don't know it. I have one but I don't know it. I don't be ringing myself, see.'

'Ok, let's try an e-mail address.'

'Oh don't be talking to be about e-mails. My son does all that but he's not here. He's in jail. I'll be goin up to him Friday if that's any good to ya?'

'Hmm... what's the address?'

'The place I left or the place I'm moving in ta now?'

'The place you're moving into now.'

'Do ye not need the address of the place I left?'

'Ok, let's try that.'

'It's in Derrypark.'

'Derrypark? Is that a town?'

'No. It's an estate.'

'And where is the estate?'

'Out the Dublin Road.'

'It's in Dublin?'

'No. Out the Dublin Road.'

'Ok. What county?'

'Athlone.'

'That's in Westmeath, isn't it?'

'Tis. I think...'

'And where in the estate is it?'

'Down the back.'

What number?

'The number fell of years ago but everyone knows where it is. It's in the corner, after where the O'Briens used ta live but they all moved out when their house got burnt...number 58.'

'58...'

'Joe knows all this. Will I just get him to ring ye again?'

'I think that would be best.'

'Ok. It won't be today because his mother is sick in hospital.'

'That's fine.'

'And it won't be tomorrow because he's bringing the car down for the NCT. The shocks are gone but he's hoping they won't notice.'

'Well, whenever he gets time should be ok.'

'I'll tell him that so.'

'Is there anything else I can help you with today?'

'No, that's grand, thanks.'

'Ok, bye. Thanks very much.'

'Bye now. Byebye, bye, bye. Thanks, bye.'

Apples And Agent Oranges

'Would you like a fried egg?'

'No thanks.'

'That's good cos the eggs are all cracked. Tea?'

'I'll chance coffee.'

'Milk?'

'Black is fine.'

'Milk is sour anyway.'

He went to the kitchen. I checked out his bookshelf. Lots of hardbacks on history and philosophy. Glue bound chunks of captured world events and thought.

Schopenhauer.

Lenin.

The Girl in the Picture.

He came back with the Maxwell House, said: 'Check if that's too hot.'

I took a belt, it tasted honest, said: 'Perfect. Thanks. I like the books.'

'Keeps me busy.'

'Good bit on Vietnam there.'

'Part of my Doctorate. Did you ever hear of Agent Orange?'

'I think so.'

'It's a herbicide. The American Army sprayed it over the University of Hawaii in the 1960's.'

'Why?'

'They wanted to see how it worked.'

'What does it do?'

'It has a lethal component called Dioxin. They were testing it out for use in Vietnam. If they could kill all the vegetation on the trees then the Vietnamese would have nowhere to hide during the bombing campaigns.'

'Did the army not know it was dangerous?'

'They did. It was proven to cause cancer, leukaemia, and horrific birth defects. They could have taken the Dioxin out and just used the plain herbicide but the process was seen to be too expensive so they just left it in. They were smart like that. Money smart.'

'I heard there's a theory now they spray mind control chemicals disguised as the exhaust fumes from airplanes.'

'Chemtrails.' He said.

'That's it, yeah.'

'Would you like a biscuit?'

'I won't, thanks.'

'Good, we don't have any anyway. Did you hear about Apple?'

'I heard they were building a factory down the road.'

'Not anymore.'

'Why not? I thought it was all planned?'

'It was. But now it's all gone to Denmark. It was the objections that put them off.'

'People didn't want it?'

'Everyone around here wanted it. Look around you, there's nothing else. The town is bypassed. Businesses are closing every ten minutes. We needed a boost. One worth 800 million euros.'

'Was it the planning?'

'The planning was accepted. Everything was fine, next thing this crowd started kicking up. People that aren't even from the area.'

'What were they protesting about?'

'Frogs and flowers and all the usual bullshit. What's a young lad supposed to do around here? There's no work, there's nothing to pass the time, no future. All he can do is emigrate. If Apple came there'd be some hope. Do you want a slice of cake?'

'No, thanks.'

'Good. It's there since Christmas. What do you think about this storm?'

'The Beast from the East?'

'Yeah. Aren't they fuckin mighty with the names too?'

'It's still awful cold but looks like the worst is over.'

'Depends.' He said.

'On what?'

'The Chemtrails. That's what's causing all this. Same as the University in Hawaii. We're all just guinea pigs. They're testing out ways to control the weather, and then they can control us using social media.'

'You don't like social media?'

'Might as well put your brain in a microwave.'

'Them iPhones have a lot to answer for.'

'They do. Sure that's all you need - *fear*. Bit of snow and a Red Alert and the whole country can be shut down. That's where they went wrong with Agent Orange.'

'Where?'

'Trying to physically control people. That's impossible. It's always been impossible. Taking over their minds is much simpler.'

My phone rang, I said: 'I better go.'

'Do you need a lift somewhere?'

'You're grand. I can walk.'

'No problem. Car's fucked by the frost anyway.'

Loughrea

Noel wanted the deal. He's a man that knows everyone, stands at pub doors, smoking and keeping an eye on the traffic. Blue jeans and brown leather jacket.

Flannel shirt. Hair greying at the side.

Smokes like he hates it.

Twenty Major man, walks down the street like a cowboy, tips of his hands in his pockets, arrogant swagger of a man that has it all solved. Likes to play the role of incisive social commentator. Like now when he says: 'Place is gone to pure fuck entirely.'

'How so, Noel?'

'Sure the bastards have it ruined.'

'Anyone in particular?'

'Don't ya know yourself now. Are you in a rush?'

'No. What about you? Working today or anything?'

'Work? Shtop. The pricks around here can't afford me.'

'What do you do?'

'Carpenter for years. But I've a truck

licence too. Are you looking to buy anythin yourself?'

'Like what?'

'I know a fella sellin bags of turf.'

'Don't need turf.'

'Let me know if you do.'

He looked over at the undertakers across the road, said: 'Fuckin funeral this evening too.'

'Anyone you know?'

'Some bollix back from America, but sure you have to be seen. Do you want a tip for a horse?'

'You're grand, thanks.'

'This is my place up here.'

We walked up a stairs. Smell like damp clothes. On the second floor there was a chinese restaurant, and a hair salon and a place that did Thai Massages. He winked here as he pulled the door back for the next flight of steps.

His place was a rooftop flat. One of four packed together for bachelors, loners and the abandoned elderly that had nowhere else to go. You could hear the town buzzing below. Cars beeping, people shouting. Church steeple in the distance. Goalposts of the football pitch. Smell of MSG from a defective extractor fan. Eons of linguistic Galway vibrating through the air.

Noel walked over to the edge, observed the horizon, waved his hand like an emperor, and said: 'Did you ever see such shite?'

'Doesn't look too bad.'

'The whole fuckin place should be burnt to the ground.'

Silence, then he said: 'Who's she?'

'Who?'

He pointed down to a girl standing against a car. She was maybe fourteen. Sixteen at best. '*Her*.' He said.

'I don't know, Noel. I don't live here.'

He frowned in recognition, said: 'She was in Lonergan's over the weekend. Gamey bit of stuff. A daughter of Ted Hughes, sold me a car one time, haype of shite too.'

He waved down with: 'Hiya....hiya...' Similar to babytalk.

She looked up, got offended, and walked off in disgust.

Noel was taken aback.

'Little bitch...' He muttered to himself, then turned back to me, said: 'See what I mean?' Anyway, the house is over here. Will this take long? I've a pint left after me on the counter. C'mon ta fuck.'

The Hippies

He was wearing a heavy suede coat and a dirty blue shirt, looked like he'd just escaped from a concentration camp. Curtains blowing in the broken kitchen window, giving a glimpse of the snow outside.

He'd been in an accident too. I know this because he said: 'I was in an accident.'

'Was it bad?'

'It wasn't my fault.'

'Someone crash into you?'

'I crashed into the back of someone else. Court next month.'

'How can you crash into someone else and it not be your fault?'

'I was drugged.'

'Who drugged you?'

'People I had living here.'

'Lodgers?'

'They were stuck for a place to stay. I felt sorry for them. So they were staying here.'

'And they drugged you?'

'At first it was little things. Stuff going missing. Money I had left out for the TV licence, and the electricity. And food from the fridge.'

'Were they locals?'

'So called *hippies*.'

'What they drug you with?'

'Some kind of horse tranquilizer.They slipped it into my tea and then asked for a lift to the dole office. By the time I got there I didn't know where I was. They had their friends waiting in a car set up and I drove straight into the back of it.'

'Were the guards called?'

'They were. Did me for drug driving.'

'What happened the hippies?'

'The hippies? Turns out they were well known for this kind of thing. They got €10,000 each for whiplash and hit the road. Haven't seen them since. And there was people here looking for them last night.'

'Guards?'

'People they owe money to.'

'Dealers?'

'Who knows?'

'What did you say to them?'

'I wasn't here. My brother was.'

'What they say to him?'

'He wouldn't answer the door.'

'Good plan.'

'Not really, they kicked it in anyway.'

'Oh.'

'So now I need a new door.'

'What happened your brother?'

'They hung him out the top window by the legs.'

'They meant business.'

'Then they dropped him.'

'Oh. Was he ok?'

'Not really. The neighbours were very annoyed. Woman next door complaining she couldn't sleep. Sure it wasn't my fault.'

'Will they be back again looking for the money?'

'You can be sure of it.'

'What'll you do?'

'They usually come at night so I sleep in a doorway downtown and I come back here during the day. My brother was caught because he wouldn't come down with me.'

'Is he going to be ok?'

'Dunno. Ambulance was here. He's in the hospital but I've no car to go over and see him. Do you find it cold here?'

'Freezing.'

'I'm going to burn an armchair later.'

'That should help.'

'Do you want tea?'

'No thanks.'

Esperanto

Her new place was the other side of the city. Posh spot where she lived on her own, or maybe she had men over. Who knew? The living room light was on and she was probably watching television, one eye towards the door, waiting for me to call. I parked up, let the pistons settle, the combustion calm down, waiting for my nerves to calibrate.

Eventually I got out, walked over. The black sky was curious, doubtful, wondering if this was a good idea. The house had double glazed windows with white frames. Turf smoke from the chimney. A traditional doorbell. Round, cream, cobwebs. I pressed it twice. Fast but not urgent. The sound landed in her hallway like a song from the biblical doom. She answered. Light brown leggings and a navy hoody. Her blonde hair in a ponytail. Smoking a Benson. She looked me up and down, said: 'You took your time.'

I shrugged, said: 'You're lucky I came at all.'

'Amin't I just? You coming in or what?'

And in she went, svelte moves. Inside, wood floor. Warm fire glowed in the corner. An aroma around the room like her neck during our lovemaking. She always had the best perfume, make a man dizzy just to pass her on the street.

I took a seat, red leather couch, she asked: 'Did you lose weight?'

'I don't think so.'

'You look good. Trim.'

'What did you want to talk about?'

Lucid blue eyes. 'Us.'

'What about us?'

Shiny olive skin. 'You still seeing that girl?'

Aoife. Immature clown. 'No. How's Dave?'

Her voice almost hoarse, like travelling over vocal rocks. 'Dave's history.'

'My heart bleeds.'

'Don't be so bitter.'

'What do you expect me to say to that?'

She threw the cigarette in the fire. It flared up for a second, then died into a spot of grey ash.

'I want to make another go of things.'

'Us?'

'No, me and the fuckin fireplace. Who do you think?'

'You want to get back together? I'm sorry if you think I'm stating the obvious, but you slept with your boss.'

'I'd like a second chance, one where I can prove I'm sorry.'

'Do you still work with him?'

'Yes.'

'See him every day?'

'Yes.'

'So what's changed?'

'You came here for a reason. If you felt so bad, you would have just stayed at home.'

'I came here to prove I was over you.'

'Liar. You're lonely. Just like me.'

'Believe what you like.'

'I believe you still love me.'

We were silent. Eventually I said: 'I waited for you all night.'

'What?'

'All night. I waited for you.'

She sighed, said: 'Let's not go there.'

'You said you'd be home at twelve, that you were tired and you wanted to start Christmas with *me* - not your workmates.'

'It was a mistake.'

'*I need a shower*. That's all you said. *I need a shower*. But I knew. I'd always known you were capable.'

'You're so dramatic.'

'And you're a whore.'

She picked up the remote control and threw it at me. It smashed behind my head, like a fireworks display of plastic buttons and small red batteries.

Pale rage, tight lips, she said: 'Don't you ever speak to me like that.'

'It's about as close to a compliment as I can get. And you never told me where it happened.'

Sarcastic aggression. '*What?*'

'You told me you slept with him, but not *where*.'

'In his house. You *know* that.'

'*Where* in his house?'

'Does it matter?'

'In the bedroom? On the floor?'

Proudly. 'In his kitchen.'

'Oh.'

'Then the bathroom.'

'Bit random.'

'Then his bedroom.'

'Did you use protection?'

'No.'

'Was it just sex?'

'No. Everything else too.'

'Did you swallow?'

'Yes. Happy?'

'Ecstatic.'

'Should I ask all the details of everyone you've ever been with?'

'Did you cum?'

'Four times.'

'A record.'

'But do I feel anything for him?'

'Do you?'

'Not a thought since it happened. I wanted to be fucked like an animal and still have *you.* I'm human. I'm sorry.'

'Did he go down on you?'

'I need that. Of course. You know I made him.'

'Did he tell his wife?'

'She doesn't care. She has a toy boy. This is

the real world, Noel. You must have been tempted to cheat too.'

'Of course.'

'Now we're getting somewhere. Honesty at last. At least I'm able to admit these things to myself.'

'Two weeks before you did it.'

Her tone was a mix of concern, relief and curious anger. 'What? Who?'

'I was out with the lads. In the club.'

'And?'

'A girl I've known for a long time. We'd never been together but I've always thought it was there, like an unsaid thing.'

'So all this time you're shoving guilt down my throat and you're just as bad?'

'Not the only thing getting shoved down your throat.'

'Mr. Witty. You should have your own shite cream van.'

'Four orgasms?'

'Long ones, too. So you spent the night with her? Mr. Moral man from the morally faithful factory.'

'We got a taxi to her place.'

'At least I told you eventually out of guilt. You're obviously a psychopath with no empathy.'

'Her house was a mess. Wine bottles, pizza boxes and clothes scattered on the floor.'

'Classy girl. Why the backstory? You slept with her or you didn't? Longest confession ever.

Jesus.'

'No, I didn't. I left again. I thought: *Why am I here in this dump?* when I have *you?*'

'Oh, so now you're a martyr to sexual abstinence. Sounds like great fun.'

'There's always a chance to walk. Except you didn't.'

'And there's always a chance to forgive someone for their mistakes. Although I'm not sure I regret it anymore.'

'You never regretted it at all.'

'You're right, except for the part where I lost you because of it. If I could have *you.* and still screw who I want, my life would be perfect.'

'Perfect?'

'I don't think about you when I masturbate, is that cheating too? What are you getting out of us *not* being together?'

'The jealousy kills me, it's like swallowing bleach.'

'At least *try* to get over it.'

'I have.'

'You're confused between sex and love. We're miserable apart, we're happy together. What's the problem?'

'What are you really asking me?'

'For understanding.'

'Polyamory?'

'Who cares if it works?'

'Because it's not pure anymore. It's contaminated with lies.'

'I confessed.'

'And dishonesty.'

'I'm being honest.'

'And infidelity.'

'Only if we're monogamous.'

'We were monogamous you fuckin fruitcake.'

'So let's not be monogamous anymore – but still have each other. People do it all over the world. It's ok. It's not a crime.'

'And what if you fall in love with someone else?'

'I've had a year, and plenty of men, and women, and both at the same time, and my feelings for you haven't changed. I love you and I can't help it. It's like a terminal illness that only makes me sick when we're apart. Have *you* met anyone else?'

'Nobody like you.'

'See? A year of our lives gone and all we had to do was flip this switch. We can go upstairs right now.'

'Now? I have to go.'

'Where?'

'I can't stay here.'

'Yes you can. And you want to.'

A note of uncertainty crept into my voice. 'No.'

'Then don't. Don't swallow your pride. I'll just ring Dave.'

'I thought he was history?'

'He can always be persuaded. If not, there's plenty of other options to keep me company.'

She had the phone out, scrolling through the contacts. I said: 'You're some bitch.'

'But I can be your bitch.' That glint of divliment in her eye and I knew I could never let her go again. No matter what the cost.

She said: 'Let's get a shower.'

'Polyamory, I don't know.'

'Just don't forbid it and I won't need to do it – as long as I know I can if I ever want to. We can live on the balance of temptation.'

'You're a bit fucked in the head.'

'Or you can just go home and have a priesty wank then.'

'No thanks.'

'Should I run the water? I miss your tongue.'

'I miss your taste.'

'I got some new toys, you'll like them.'

Silence, atoms of the future assembling into a concrete form, like a new emotional constitution. I said: 'Maybe just tonight then, and see how it goes.'

'I agree. You have a record to beat.'

The White House

Wind blew sharp, like razor blades you couldn't see. And the Polish mechanic had blue overalls, a missing front tooth, and a worried look. And the bonnet of the car was open, like a mouth frozen in horror with an engine inside. And the temperature had been going up, and the innards had made strange noises, like a skeleton with the shakes from drink.

In fear of eternal silence, I said: 'What do you think?'

He put his hand on the radiator, thought for a second, and went: 'Hmm....I think this engine is about to die.'

'I wouldn't go that far now.'

'Your car is old.'

'But well kept.'

'It might be a faulty switch.'

'That sounds more positive.'

'Then again, could be the oil pump.'

'Still better than a dead engine?'

'Big job all the same.'

'How big?'

'We'll have to take down the sump.'

I nodded, like I knew what that meant, then

said: 'Can you do it today?'

'Very busy. Everybody want. Tomorrow.'

'Bring it in tomorrow?'

'Yes. Tomorrow. Day after today.'

'Will it break down before then, or can I keep driving it?'

'Keep driving. No problem. No breakdown.'

So I drove off, delighted with the all clear, like a bridal car with tin cans tied to the back, rattling up the road.

Later, when it broke down, I pulled into an estate to see what could be done. I got out and opened the bonnet again and looked inside. Maybe there'd be an obvious pipe unhooked, or a lead disconnected, or it might just need water. After a few seconds, I stood back and looked around, maybe fate might intervene. And Spring vaguely threatened, and birds sang uncertain, and daylight lingered, like a haunted echo of more innocent times.

There was a white house across the road and you could see a family through the front window, all huddled around an open fire. Then the front door opened and a girl came out and asked: 'Are you ok?'

She had long hair, the colour of rust, and tight black jeans and a beige velvet blouse. A young face but with the pain of a wounded soul and her eyes were rheumy and bloodshot.

'Car broke down.'

'Is it bad?' Something in her voice had the

song of a suffocated helper. A teacher in another life, or a nurse maybe, a bright lit room locked behind dead possibility but here she was, helping.

'Not great, I think. It might just need water.'

'I'll get you some. Come in.'

I went in. Followed her to the kitchen. Don't mind the mess she goes, hoarse, different personalities competing to break through.

School books and half-eaten dinners left around. A full ashtray and a tremendous smell of weed. Suddenly there was a shout from the sitting room. Man's voice. 'Laura! What the fuck're you at?'

'Helpin this fella?'

'With what?'

'Givin him water for his car.'

'Fuck him! Tell him to get his own fuckin water!'

'Shut up, you.' Then she turned to me, said: 'That's Paddy. Never mind him.'

'You're grand, I'll go again. Water probably won't make much difference.'

She handed me a porcelain jug, worn paint on cracked fingernails, a scent like mango and honey, said: 'Here. Take this anyway.'

'I'll drop it back when I'm finished.'

She went back into the sitting room, saying at the same time: 'Paddy, will you ever shut up when there's people here.'

I was walking to the car but I could still hear them shouting through the window.

'Who's *people*? What are you letting strangers in for?'

'He wanted water for his car.'

'You're an awful stupid bitch.'

'Don't you be calling me a....'

'And what if he's from the drug squad?'

'With a broke down car?'

'That's the way they work you clown.'

'The only clown here is *you*.'

'I'll fuckin burst his head if he comes back here again.'

'You wouldn't burst eggs you lazy lump of shite.'

'I'll kill him stone dead.'

'Stop fighting!' Screamed a young girl. Then there was a sound like a table got flipped over, and a glass smashed, and Laura screaming. 'Leave me alone ya fuckin bollix!'

'I'm gettin Uncle Eddie!' Shouted the child and she ran out the door, and across the estate with small black shoes, and her pony tail bouncing like a hare chased by greyhounds.

'I'm sick of tryin to get sense in to your thick head full of stones.' Shouted Paddy.

I had the feeling he was pulling her hair. I looked down at the engine. There was a smell of burnt oil and liquorice. I topped up the water but it didn't really need any so I put the cap back on and walked over with the jug. Maybe Paddy would attack me instead now and I could break it on his face.

Laura had escaped into the hall, shouting: 'You're a bastard, nothin but a bastard, a useless dopey, fat lazy gud for nathin bastard.'

'C'mon in here again and I'll fuckin kill ya.'

'You're only a coward of a waster nobody bastard, don't be annoying me.'

She saw me coming, pulled her hair back, said: 'Sorry about that. Is the car ok?'

'Yeah, should be grand now. Thanks.'

She sniffled, her voice breaking, holding back the tears, asked: 'Would you like a cup of Miwadi or anythin?'

Jimmy Connolly

John said: 'Thanks, will you call up to my brother Martin?'

'I will, what number's he in?'

'23. He's looking for a change, too.'

I got to 23. Martin signed up, said: 'Will you call to my brother Paddy?'

'I will. What number is he in?'

'24. Next door.'

I got to 24. Paddy signed up, said: 'Will you call to my brother Jimmy.'

'I will, what number is he in?'

'25. Next door.'

I got to 25. Jimmy said: 'Is it a good deal?'

'Tis.'

'Show it to me.'

I showed it to him and he said: 'That's a fuckin good deal. Come on inside.'

Inside. Torn couch. Smell of spilled cider. Dead modem in the corner

I said: 'I'll sign you up so?'

'Do, but...what kind of details do you want?'

'Basic.'

'Do you need account numbers? From banks?'

'No.'

'And say if there was a fella that was signed

up with ye before, like, and he ran up a big debt...'

'It probably wouldn't go through. Or you'd get a bill for the money owed.'

'Oh.'

'Do you owe anything?'

'Eh....no. I don't think so. Will you need ID if I sign up?'

'No, just your name and phone number. And address. Paddy and Martin went for it too....sure you might as well.'

'Who's Paddy and Martin?'

'Your brothers.'

'Oh, they're not my brothers.'

'No?'

'No.'

'Well, Paddy said to call up to his brother in 25. This is 25, isn't it?'

''Tis, but, I don't know them people at all. They must be mixed up. Can you sign me up so?'

'Right so. What's your name?'

'Eh...Jimmy.'

'Jimmy....?'

'Hmmm....Connolly.'

'Ok, Jimmy Connolly. And we have the address here. And what's your number?'

He rhymed off the first few digits that came into his head. After I asked: 'And date of birth, Jimmy?'

'Does it have to be mine?'

'Preferably.'

'Eh....28.10.1964.'

He looked about 35 so I said: 'You look good

for a man pushin 60.'

'I do keep myself well.'

'Ok, good man. E-mail address?'

'Yeah, here.'

'No that's a postcode.'

'Oh, right. Are they not the same thing?'

'Not really.'

'I don't have one so.'

'Sound. Nearly there anyway.'

'Do you want a smoke?' He asked.

'No, thanks.'

'Do you mind if I have one?'

'Go ahead, sure.'

'These are fags I bought for €5 from a Pakie lad up the road.'

'Good price.'

'Do you know anyone looking to buy any?'

'Not at the moment.'

'Let me know if you do. They're supposed to be full of rat poison but I don't believe that. Sure people'd tell you anything now.'

'They would. Ok, we're done here.'

'Good stuff.'

'Just need you to sign.'

'No problem. Where do I sign?'

'Bottom line there.'

'What name do I put down?'

'Your own name. The name you gave me.'

He blinked and looked at me blankly.

'Jimmy Connolly.' I said.

'Oh, yeah, Jimmy Connolly. That's right.

That's me.'

He took the pen, and wrote *Jimmy*, then looked up and asked: 'How do you spell Connolly?'

Side Jobs

She lived in an estate with rusted gates and junk in all the lawns. Her place was down the back, in the corner, with flaked paint and high grass. We knocked, winter evening coming fast, bruised twilight and sky lesions. Inside, there was quiet, then a sound like someone almost tripped over a box, followed by a voice. It was soft and young, tainted with a smoker's song of confrontation. Maybe we were inspectors of some kind? TV licence, debts, here with a warrant or a summons, maybe worse. Knocks were rarely good news.

'What's it ye want?'

We told her. She said OK, but she couldn't open the front door, the kids had lost the keys.

I said we could climb in the window.

'No, come around the back and I'll let ye in.'

There was more tripping, moving things around, legs of wooden tables screeching on stone floors.

We walked by the dirty gable towards the garden. A smell everywhere like open fires and polluted smoke from things that shouldn't be burnt – nappies, plastic bottles, polythene. Chimney's proudly pumping out their black death the whole way down the street.

The back door was boarded up with thick slabs of timber. It took her a while to get them all down. Inside, the kitchen was dark, glaucoma scene, and there was bare tungsten wires where the lightbulbs used to be.

'I'm sorry it's so dark in here. Waiting for the landlord to fix them bulbs.' She said.

We stepped in. Torn lino, a smell like mould, an out of commission cooker and a rusty sink.

'I'm Sarah.' She said.

She was young, about 22. Tight blue jeans and a red jacket. A long black mane of thick hair, thin lips, and brown eyes. She had her arms folded across a black lace top, taking command, said: 'Sorry again about the state of the place. The hole is out this way. Walk with me here through the sitting room.'

More dim light. A cheap bulb, maybe 15 watts, makes you feel uncertain, like the electricity isn't fully committed, might get bored and die at any second. And there was clothes drying on a laundry rack. Kids pyjamas, tiny vests, underwear. And a smell like damp shoes and stale bread. Old worn carpet, cigarette butts, and deep dark stains from spilled wine, maybe beer, maybe blood? Toys with missing parts. That teddy with no arm, the tractor with no wheel, bits of mixed up board games in a plastic box.

Sarah said: 'I'm not long moved in. I thought you were here to install the internet.'

'No, not us. Are you waiting for an engineer?'

'Yeah, the internet and the channels. Getting myself set up, finally.'

'Were you gone somewhere?'

'I'm just out of rehab. I was an addict.'

'You're young.'

'Started at 14. Heroin.'

We let that settle. And the walls were red and sparsely populated with cheap surrealist art. Marylin Monroe beside a Russian General and Che Guevara holding an AK47. And a black man reading a bible, and a horse with a dog's head, and a cat reading the communist manifesto. Suddenly, the November night took a bite through the window, a stealthy panther, always prowling for the weakest link, silent crystals of cold penetrating like tiny arrows of sharp ice.

'Waiting on oil, too.' She said.

The light dimmed for a second, then came back, and I asked: 'Did you get a good deal on the internet?'

'€25 a month, but it'll probably go up then after a while. Do you want tea?'

'You're grand, thanks. Where's the hole in the wall?'

'It's over here. I'll show you.'

We walked into the hall. Cold. Stone floor, decadent breeze like a dead man's wheeze. A howl from dead generations of bad insulation. And that smell again, like old damp towels.

On the ground there was an unwired socket. Screws and screwdrivers left around like a half-built thing. Above it was a big hole in the shabby plasterboard wall. It had the terrified look of a toothless man about to get hit with something huge.

Sarah stood beside me, looking at it, pharmacy grade perfume, a tester maybe, a scent like nostalgia for innocence, lovers on a carefree night, that decade she never had.

'Landlord tried to do it himself.' Said Sarah.

'Do what?' I asked her.

'Wire the plug. But he got a big shock off it and started shouting. And then he kicked the wall and put the big hole in it and left.'

'This won't take us long. But there'll still be a call out charge.'

'I don't mind, he's paying for it anyway.'

'We'll throw a few bulbs in the kitchen too.'

'Thanks. That'd be great.'

We started with the socket, gathered up the bits, getting it done right.

Sarah stood watching, arms still folded. Then she said: 'Sorry again you had to come around the back. That's a new door and the last one was kicked in.'

'By who?'

'Dealers. Said I owed them money, wanted me to prostitute myself to pay it off.'

'They know where you live and everything?'

'They live across the road themselves. I grew up around here. We all did. You'd be walkin down the street and one of the girls would be like: "Hey, Sarah, do you want to go halves on a bag?" and I'm like "No, I'm off it." And it's all like how come? and why....? And all that. You know?'

She liked having someone to talk to, from somewhere else. I said: 'That can't be easy.'

'It's not. I was off it a few times before but never properly, ya know? I always went back cos there was no choice, like what else is there to do?'

'Have ya many kids?'

'Two, they keep me goin. Once we get set up here I'll keep myself to myself.'

'Just yourself, is it?'

'Yeah, they come from two different fathers but one's in Glasgow hiding from the guards cos he tried to rob a post office and the other fella died last year.'

'Sorry to hear that.'

'Don't worry. I'm not sorry. He used to bate me black and blue.'

'How'd he die?'

'The priest killed him.'

'The priest?'

'Yeah, no. Like, the priest was drivin down the road and he had a heart attack and lost control of the car and ran him over.'

'Did the priest die too?'

'No, he's fine. Still sayin mass. I do thank him every time I see him.'

The socket was ready and I tested it and it worked. 'That's your plug fixed anyway.'

'Mighty, thanks. Don't know why the other clown of a landlord couldn't do it right.'

'What's he like?'

'A bollocks. Wanted sex for rent. I told him to fuck off. Do ye like this job?'

I started with the filler, measured the hole, probably need a new slab.

Job's grand, I said, we get to meet all sorts.

'I'm sure ye do. I'm on the council list for a proper place.'

'Are ya long waiting?'

'About three years. We were in my mothers, then here, so hopefully next year we'll have a right house.'

'Please God.'

I'm startin a course next week too.'

'In what?'

'Social care.I want to help people like myself, ya know?'

More bits of the wall gave way, making the hole even bigger. I said: 'He gave this wall a fair kick.'

'Oh, he's an animal. Has a few places around here. And this is the best of them.'

Boom Time Auctioneer

The auctioneer was in a brown suit and glasses that made him look like a surprised owl. He looked up at the house, said: 'This is a good one. Good location.'

'What's good about the location?'

'Close to schools, bus routes, motorways and the neighbours are ok. You go to some places, I'll tell ya, you wouldn't put a dog in them.'

'And what about the people that own it, why do they want to sell it?'

'They want to sell this one and build another one.'

'Why do they want to do that?'

'They reckon they can sell this one for about €400,000 and then build the other one for about €250,000 and keep the difference.'

'Where they building the new one?'

'*Here*.'

'*Here*?'

'*Here*.'

'Where?'

'Here in the garden.'

'*This* garden?'

'Yeah. See....you'd be buying the house

alright, but they're not selling the garden. So there'd be a construction site here while you're moving in. Still a good price for it. Bout as good as ye'll get in this market. *The Celtic Tiger* ain't going anywhere I'm afraid....'

'Is there anything else we can look at?'

He frowned, thought, and said: 'There's one other place alright, but the woman living there is a bit mad.'

'What's wrong with her?'

'Whore for the drink.'

'Does she want to sell?'

'She thinks she does, but who knows? Sure she's half cracked.'

'Has anyone made any offers on it?'

'I had a couple there last week. They seemed interested but I don't think it's going to work out.'

'Why not? Is there something wrong with the house itself?'

'No, nothing like that.'

'Can't afford it?'

'Not that either, no. They were a nice couple. *Well off.* Young. She was a teacher. Blondie one. Real tall and good looking. He's in the bank. Up from Galway, looking to settle here for a few years.'

'What's the price?'

'€280,000.'

'Not bad. What went wrong?'

'Ah sure wasn't I going showing it to them anyway, and I had your one living there told to be gone, but was she fuck gone? She was still there when we landed, half pissed, givin us dirty looks like we were trespassing. And she in her pyjamas and the hair standing on her head. She was the cut out of *Beetlejuice.* Anyway, I pulled her aside and told her to fuck off up the stairs until we were finished. She was thick enough but up she went. Do ye smoke?'

'No thanks.'

He lit a major and continued. 'Anyway, I brought this couple around. The kitchen, the sitting room, outside into the garden. They were asking decent questions. It wasn't going too bad. And we were standing there talking anyway and next thing I heard the toilet flushing upstairs.'

'So?'

'I remembered all of a sudden that you weren't supposed to flush it. The pipe that was supposed to bring all the waste down the drain was gone from the wall.'

'So what happened?'

'I turned to look up and sure next I knew a big plop of a shite fell down on my head. For fuck's sake, I didn't know what to do. It was warm and it smelled like onions, and stale meat and....and... pissy red wine. The young blondie one got sick straight away and your man pulled her out the door and that's the last I heard of them. Had to buy a new suit after it.'

He finished the cigarette and continued. 'We can take a look at the place if you want. If that bitch is there though, she'll play fuck....I wouldn't fancy it.'

Dylan Went Electric

Dylan went electric about 3.30am. On the broad American streets when I meet this doll, this doll that looks like an actress, and the night above was like black cider and ice cube vodka stars. Tim Horton's throbbing to the left and the cabs like fireflies in the commercial night. She hailed one, all style and movie moves. Got to her place. To a smell of laundry, cosmetics, youth and confidence. Shoes and a desk and scattered clothes. Found a swivel chair and sailed across the wood floor. Click go the clack wheels through the bright lights and the alarm clock ticking towards the crazy dawn. Dylan went electric and JFK fell at the hands of Lee Harvey and Martin Luther King sang truth and the cider's roaring loud.

On the floor, after more Jack Daniels and coke, she tasted like lip balm and cigarettes as we celebrated the silence and the colours of night. Till the sun came up and sang through the watery windows. And in the dawn blue after. Her face was something serene and then it was time to leave. Something about a landlord. A new place and keys and the squeaky wheels on the clattery train of life. On the street there was combustion and noise and morning and the heavy future. And oh, sweet America, all machines and concrete and no soul. Traffic passed. She smoked some more. Striking features and rain drops and grey distant clouds. At the loud junction we attempted a goodbye, and we kissed, all passion and roaring desire as we stole a moment from the rusty fabric of time. Then she really had to go and she gave me her number and said to call but it stole something from the dream and we both knew it so we wished adios and turned away, and away some more, and some more. But walking home, the rain didn't feel that bad. Maybe it was the Red Bull or the Jack Daniels or both. People waited at bus stops and there were gardens with families and big cars and elegant houses. And I thought what a world, what a show. Wondered what time the pubs opened in America. And how Dylan went electric and JFK fell at the hands of Lee Harvey. And now this rusty millennium, dodging wet American cracks on Sunday mornings, bloodstream vodka and shivers like cold, or the coward fear trying to muster a shaking threat. Later at the bar, somewhere on Commercial Drive, drinking cider and flashbacks of abandon and surrender. Her ghost haunting me, hovering, whispering across the back of my neck. And the cider tastes good, like liquid gold. And there's a guy on his own with a notebook and a blue pen. Oh, you can feel it, kid. The scrape of that ink. The words that'll make all the difference. The collection of images, the rhyming meter and the crowd of applause and appreciation. You can hear it, can't ya? That commentator saying how you saw it coming, called the world on social collapse. How 'bout those notes, maybe we could put 'em together, send them somewhere. Tap that pen. Tap it loud. Cos the dream is close, sometimes the dream is so close, the shivers rain hard and you can almost touch it, the elusive truth, and then others; the shot rings out and JFK falls at the hands of Lee Harvey and down goes the balloon. Maybe you saw Martin Luther march with solidarity and courage. Saw the napalm fall across Hanoi, watched the footage of the blood-stained Irish Catholics cry. Some men say it's the whisper of Karl Marx, breathing across history, others say it's the wrath of God. Some men pay their taxes and watch TV and don't think it's anything at all. You find answers in the night, you and your pen and the neon light, you and the burn of the waitresses' eyes, and the game called something's missing, something's wrong, there's a vacuum here, a lonely song. Watch those pages accumulate, build a wall, build it against death, build it high before it's too late. But don't worry, kid, you got it covered. You and the blanket of dark cider and the ice cube vodka stars. That electric possible sky. Oh, sweet America, all machines and concrete and no soul. And lip balm and cigarettes and the colours of night.

The Midget Stripper

The supervisor was partial to a hot chocolate and a power trip. He took a sip, pulled rhetorical with: 'You *lost* your jacket?'

'Yeah.'

'How?'

'It wasn't there when I woke up this morning.'

'You know you need that, right? You can't work without it. It's *policy*. You need to talk to Craig. He's in the office.'

I walked into the office and Craig was there. Red standard issue jacket, curly hair, tanned, somewhere in his fifties. He was reading an article in a local paper. He gave it a second for dramatic pause, like he was just reaching the end and didn't want to be interrupted. After, he put it down, asked: 'What?'

'I lost my jacket.'

'You *lost* your jacket? What? How? Where?'

'I was looking for a midget pole dancer. She was supposed to be there last night and...'

He closed the paper, went: 'What? WAIT.... back up...'

I told him they were doing *Two-for-One*

vodkas down in the Ocean Port. It was a dark blue place with a pole in the middle and lots of shifty types with baseball caps and flannel shirts. There was a pool table too but it didn't work half the time and the tips of the cues were always gone so when you hit a ball it made a sound like breaking teeth. And there was a rumour about a midget dancer and she was supposed to be there last night. I was about to tell him I was also working as a journalist, doing an article about it, but he cut me off with an incredulous: 'Christ, are all Irish guys this stupid?'

'I don't know. I can't speak for them all.'

'So what do you need?'

'A jacket.'

Sigh. 'What colour?'

'Orange.'

'Ok, you look about extra-large. We should have some here somewhere.'

'Thanks.'

'This could be a security threat, you know?'

'I know.'

'I mean, what if some guy comes in wearing *your* jacket and tries to steal somethin...'

'Well at least it's extra-large so it won't fit the midget if she tries to rob the place.'

'Don't get smart, buddy. You're in enough trouble as it is.'

I looked down at the paper. He'd been reading an article I'd written myself a week before. My name and picture beside it. I'd covered a hockey game for the Olympics but Craig still hadn't made the connection. I know this because he said: 'Actually, I don't even know who you are, how the hell can I just give you a jacket because you walk in here and say you want one?'

'I have a security pass.'

Sarcasm central here with: 'Eh, can I see it?'

'Here.'

He looked at it. Good scan. Frowned. Looked at me like a guard at an airport with a passport. He handed it back with another tired sigh, like he was satisfied. 'Ok, there might be one in the cupboard over there.'

'Over here?'

'No, the top one there. It says *jackets*. Do you think you can handle that?'

'Oh, right.'

I took one down, opened up the plastic and said: 'I'll put it on here so, in case I get mugged or somethin on the way out and someone steals this one too.'

'That's a good idea, and no strip joints with this one, ok?'

'Ok.'

He took back the paper, started reading, laughed a bit. Mostly ignored me. When I had the jacket on, he looked up and went. 'Fits you.'

'Thanks. Enjoyin the paper?'

'Yeah.' He pointed at my article, with my name and picture beside it and sincerely asked: 'Have you read this guy?'

'No.'

'He's good, smart, funny. I like his style.'

'I'll keep an eye out for him.'

'Do that. And you're on the clock, I'm docking you fifteen minutes for this, get out of here.'

'Right so. Bye now.'

Cidona Life

The fella at the counter was bored. Looking around. Tapping beermats. Eyeing up the barmaid. He picked up his phone and dialled. The other side answered and he said: 'Hello, yeah, Larry? Luke here, how's things, yeah, I'm good, changed my number there lately, sorry, couldn't pay the bill! I'm here in the pub. Will you come in for one? Oh, you're workin? You're on lunch? Right, sound, how's the job goin? Yeah, sound, ok, no bother, talk to ya.'

He hung up. Looked around some more. Dialled again.

'Hello, yeah, Tom? How's things? Luke here, different number.... you comin into the Skeff for one? You had another kid? Oh right, with the same burd? Nice. Fair play, man, delighted for ya... you're not comin for one so, to celebrate? Oh right, I get ya...yeah, yeah, yeah...sound....am I workin myself? No, ah...things went quiet there lately, so they had to let a few lads go, and between that now and missin the odd Monday, you know yourself, they were glad to see the back of me I'd say! I'm lookin into a few things though, there's a fella supposed to ring me now next week. And I crashed the car, did ya hear that? No? No, I'm ok, bit of whiplash alright so waiting on a few pound for that...oh you're busy? Go on, go on, go on....see ya, Tom, thanks.'

He put the phone on the counter. Took a sip of his cider. Rubbed his knee. Looked over at me. I was reading a book. Hoping he wouldn't talk. The barmaid came to the rescue, asked him if he wanted another. He had three quarters of a Bulmers left, but went: 'Go on so, sure.'

He dialled another number. It answered. 'Jane? Howya, how's things? Luke here, new number, changed networks there lately, what're you up ta? Yeah, yeah, I'm in town alright, yeah, you around? I'm in the Skeff? What am I doin? I'm havin a pint! Oh yeah, I'm back on it. Did you not hear? No, no, I was off it for a while alright, but then, ah...it was July and it was comin up to the races in August, so I said I'd have a few, then sure the races came and I kept goin til my birthday in October and sure next thing it was Christmas, and ah...you know yourself, with Paddy's Day coming up now and everything, but ah, how's life with you? Oh, you've to go? That's himself in the background is it? Sound sound...talk soon, oh, Jane? I meant to say to ya...hello? Hello? Jane? Shite.'

He took the phone away from his ear and scowled like the reception gods had cut him off. The barmaid came with the drink. He gulped down the pint that wasn't finished and took the fresh one, then handed her a fiver. She went to the till, put it through, came back with a few cents change and left it on the counter. He took it gladly, asked her: 'What time are you finished?'

She rolled her eyes, said: 'Don't even bother.'

And she walked off. He tried to smile. Looked around for support.

I was the only one there. He said: 'What's that you're readin?'

'Dostoyevsky.'

'Oh, is it any good?'

'It's not bad.'

'What's it about?'

'Russia.'

'Oh, right. Them Russians are daft bastards.'

'They are, yeah.'

'Is it about the Mafia, is it?'

'No.'

'Who was your man with the big pink mark on his head that time, looked like an egg with glasses?'

'I don't know.'

'Mussolini, was it?'

'That was him, yeah.'

'He was mental.' He leaned over, picked up the edge of the book. 'Is there many pages in it?'

'A good few.'

'Did you ever read the Roy Keane book?'

'No.'

'Unreal. He was dead right to leave Saipan that time. Where are you from yourself?'

'Mayo.'

'Oh MAYO! For fuck's sake…do you want a pint?'

'No, thanks.'

'What's that you're drinkin?'

'Cidona.'

'Oh, not much a Cidona man myself. Fell off the wagon there lately.'

'How's that goin for ya?'

'More like somersaulted off the fuckin thing. It's grand sure, bitta craic…could be worse. Here I'll get you one of them, where's this bitch gone? Face on her would turn milk sour.'

'You're alright. I've to go anyway.'

He got all offended with: 'Where ya goin?'

'Somewhere else.'

'Aragh, fuck ya so.'

'G'luck.'

He picked up the phone. Could hear him on the way out with: 'Hello? Gerry? Yeah, how's things? Luke here, new number. You're where? Australia? What the fuck're you doin there?'

Psychology In The Taxi

Rang the taxi.

He arrived ten minutes later. Black Opel *Insignia.*

I sat in. A smell like farts and air fresheners.

He put it in first, moved a bit, asked me where I was going.

Moustache.

Huge stomach.

I told him I had a psychology exam in the tennis courts in Salthill.

He shrugged and drove on. Didn't say anything for a while, just gave an odd glance at the papers and books I was trying to cram before we got there.

Eventually he broke the silence with: 'Did you ever get the shits, did ya?'

'The shits?'

'Yeah, a dose of the shits, fuck me, I got them once. Had a horse runnin and I got awful excited and next thing my fuckin hole opened. Thank fuck there was a jacks close by, had to sit on the fuckin thing for nearly half an hour...'

'Right, did the horse win?'

'Did it fuck. Sure, if it wasn't for bad luck, I'd have no luck.'

I kept reading, giving no invitation for talk, trying to digest Freud, Skinner, Jung, and Spearman's Row. Then he said: 'Will you pass that test do you think?'

'Hopefully, just tryin to cram a few last bits in here.'

'Christ,what's the women like out there?'

'Where?'

'In the college. I rode a bird myself last Sunday mornin...fuckin dirty bitch.'

'Lovely.'

'I picked her up there, not far from your house, she was down from Dublin, after stayin the night in some local fella's place, said the men down here are no good at all and she didn't get a proper ride the night before. Fuckin ragin she was, after comin all the way down.'

'Sounds like an awful tragedy alright.'

'Well,anyway, she was kinda lookin me up and down and she says, "You're probably a proper man alright," she says. I says I am, I fuckin am, why wouldn't I be? "There's a later train," she goes, "I could get that" I says how do you mean? "Pull in somewhere," she says. So, I found a quiet sideroad and I pulled in and up she hopped and took out my flute and, fuck me, we nearly broke the seat here. Thought she was goin to paralyze herself off the steerin wheel at one stage. Anyway, I gave her a good goin over and she was happy then, you know? Went home *happy*. "You're the fella I was lookin for alright," she goes, "And where were *you* last night?" Any time, says I, ring the fuckin number. "Maybe," she says, "that'll do for now, but you never know when you might see me down here again."

So, I dropped her back at the train and she fucked off and that was it. Christ, the fuckin women'd crack your head, wouldn't they?' Beat, then. 'Psychology now, what's that about?'

'It's the study of the human mind.'

'Do you know much about it?'

'I hope so. There's 400 people doin the exam and only the top 26 go through to next year.'

He gave me a good long look, narrowly missed a cyclist, exhaled loudly through his nose, and said: 'You're probably fucked so.'

'Thanks.'

'Does this place have a jacks out here?'

'I don't know.'

'Them fuckin books are awful big.'

'I s'pose they are.'

'I hope you don't get the shits anyway. Can you look into the other fella's copy beside you if you don't know the answers? That's what I used to do...'

'They have the tables too far apart.'

He sniffed and tutted. 'Ah, sure they've copped on to everything now, can't get away with anythin anymore. I'm just finished myself, did the night shift, home now for the breakfast and shleep for the day. Here we are now.'

He pulled in and yawned. The meter said €8.60. Then he pressed a button and it went up to €10.75 and he said: 'A tenner'll do, thanks.'

El Niño

Her name was El Niño. Her father called her that because the night she was born there was a storm. He said it signified the way she was to live her life. I met her in an elevator. I wanted to go three floors and forget about it. Instead, everything changed.

Thing is, bout meeting a girl like her, it hits you like a curve ball. It's not like you get written notice. It's fast, short, and leaves you spinning. I left my finger on the button and asked: 'Goin up?'

'Third Floor.'

'Arts?'

'Yeah, second year.'

It was the last day of the semester and I'd spent it following a lecturer around. I'd been after him for a while. His wallet bulged so big I coulda jumped up right there in the class and taken him out. But that's the downfall. That's how mosta my friends spend their holidays in a cage. They get impatient, can't wait, always want the big scoop.

The guy taught socialism. Hardliner. I disagreed. What a fuckin hypocrite. I looked down. Saw this wad popping out, thought: fuck, I gotta get me some of that. We all like the extra capital. But I waited. Scoped him out. Asked him a question after, like: 'Excuse me, Mr. McKenna? I'm just wonderin where can I get a copy of *The Communist Manifesto?*'

He looked me up and down said: 'Call into my office this afternoon. I'll have one there. Costs €3.50.'

Thought: Fuck you, selling the goddamn pamphlet that says we should kill the capitalist. Makes me sick. He bent over to get his briefcase. I saw a chance. Thought about it. Then some chick came from behind and said: 'Sorry, Mr. McKenna? Do you have a minute?'

Ah, fuck off hippy kids, always looking for the revolution. I'd nearly scored too. Heart beating fast, going in for the kill and snared. Bitch didn't even know what she was talking about, just trying to sound all smart and shit.

Left. Thought: G*et him later.* Maybe at the office. Send him somewhere.

Started the game ten years ago. Never been caught, except once. My father clocked me hitting some geyser on his way to the post office. Pension hanging out. I was in fast, hit hard, knocked him. Played the Good Samaritan, pulled him up with one hand, took his cash with the other. Next thing I see is sky. Father staring down, frothing at the mouth. *Give it back*, he says, *ya thief. Never been no robbin in this family until now, and I'll knock it outta ya...*

He had a heart attack six months later. Tough times. Needed to bring home some grade.

Took up robbing again. Probably turn in his grave, but, what're ya gonna do? Get a fuckin job?

The elevator hit the first floor. I took in her intoxicating perfume, asked: 'You doin English?'

She went for casual and arty with: 'Classics and Soc/Pol. You?'

'English and Soc/Pol. Goin go see McKenna, about buyin *The Communist Manifesto.*'

'Oh, were you in that lecture today?'

'Yeah, bullshit or what?'

'I thought it was interesting.'

'Whatever you're into.'

'Why you want the manifesto then?'

I shrugged, said: 'I wanna take a read over the summer. Give it a chance, see if this Marx kat's really got anything to say.'

'What about the revolution? Wasn't that enough?'

'Maybe, but I wasn't around, so now I gotta find out for myself.'

'You tell McKenna?'

'No, bastard wants €3.50. Tells me he wants a revolt against the capitalist, but I gotta pay for it. Fuck that.'

She raised her eyebrows. Style and attitude, said: 'It's all about progress.'

'Or a lost cause.'

'Or the bigger picture?'

'Or floor three. Beauty before the beast, babe.'

'Interesting ride.'

'Went too fast. Gimme your number and we'll take it up later.'

'You don't waste time.'

'Life is short and the clock is tickin.'

She scribbles it out, says: 'I'll let you buy me a drink, see how it works from there.'

'I'm honoured.'

'Name's *El Niño.*'

'El Niño?'

'There was a storm the night I was born. My father said it signified the way I would live my life.'

'I'm Charlie. After my father, and my grandfather, and his old man too. One long line of Charlie.'

She smiled a hundred suns, said: 'Cute, see you this evening?'

I walked off with the feel of her wallet inside my coat. Silly bitch. Wrote the number and left her bag open. What was I supposed to do? Sorry Mr. Opportunity, nobody around?

Got to his office. He was bald with a gut. Sat typing something. Probably more overpriced communism. Knocked, said: 'Mr. McKenna? I talked to you today, after your lecture, about buying *The Communist Manifesto?*'

He turned, fixed his glasses and scrutinized. Obvious disdain. Must have been my clothes. Brown leather jacket, loose long shirt. Baseball cap on backwards.

'Yes, yes...Marxist economics, wasn't it?'

'Yeah.'

I looked around. Saw books on Orwell, Nietzsche, Smith, Rawls, Hobbes, Locke, Rousseau. The whole fuckin crew. Oscar winning irony. What a phony, with the belly and the big shiny watch on his hairy wrist.

He ruffled in the desk, took out a copy. 'Well Mr...'

'Charlie.'

'Well, Charlie. That's €3.50, please.'

Took out my stash, asked: 'You got change for a hundred?'

He frowned and I saw the disappointment. The dilemma. The profit or *the cause*? Checks his pockets, looks around. Says: 'I...let me see, I... don't... at the moment. Anything smaller?'

'Nope.'

'Oh.'

Frown time for me. 'Oh?'

'Tell you what, you can call back with... no, actually...hang on and I'll see if Doris is in the office. She might have some.'

Disco. He took his fat ass up and waddled out. Almost caused a tremor on the corridor. This place is a real fuckin Jurassic Park. Scanned the office some more. Saw the wallet on the table. Could be obvious. Fuck it, not here for the socialism. Acted fast, skimmed the notes, left a few. Didn't want him seeing the wad all thin. These guys looked after nothing better than dust. Heard him thank Doris. Probably fuckin her. Blowjob at lunch. Some extra bonus cash on the side. Some revolution.

He returned. 'Yes, got some change from Doris. A hundred you say?'

'Aye, captain.'

We did the exchange. The cold greasy feel of money changing paws. The fear that someone's gonna snap the goods and screw the whole deal. This could get ugly. Everyone just be like Fonz and stay cool. I took the pamphlet and watched him, like a starved dog, stuff the cash into his sweaty pocket and smile. Yellow teeth, stink of cigars. Wet armpits.

He stood salivating, jingling coins, said: 'You'll like it.'

'Oh yeah. Can't wait to get a read of this. I've been after it for a while now. I love Marx. He's my hero.'

He turned his back and dismissed me with: 'His day will come again.'

I left and took the lift back down. Could still smell El Niño. Her scent in the atmosphere, like an erotic angel. In my head, I had an image of McKenna. Sitting in his office, with a smile for another one recruited to his illusions. And behind him, an ugly sceptre, hanging with menace, waiting to sever his spine. And the wallet lying open, gutted like a slaughtered animal. At least he got €3.50 back. I threw the book in the bin and walked home.

-

She looked beautiful in the photograph. Sallow, and those hazel eyes, that tell you she understands almost everything, like she can see into your soul. Necklace, colourful beads, and that blinding smile. She had the usual. Cards, a license, receipts. Some looked sentimental, others just there. Most important was the cash. Counted hers and the stack from the Marxist. Made the day handsome. She must have been paying fees or something. Sat back and my bed creaked. Outside, it was bright as the church bells rang for six. Still had her number and I was tempted to call. Monday was a bad night on the street. No crowd, no anonymity, no action. I picked up her wallet and shoved it in an envelope. It's an honour thing, and a karma thing too. Always have to post the wallet back. Every time, get the money and send home the rest. Just coz, keeps us in business. Poor fools fill it up again so the next guy can hit 'em.

An hour of bored contemplation passed. Then I hit the dial style. She sounded weird on the phone. Her voice all smooth and soft, like warm strawberry milk.

'Hey, storm girl. Wanna get that drink?'

'Sorry, Pablo, broke like a train wreck.'

'No way, kitten. How you gonna cause a hurricane at home?'

'No dust, honey. No choice.'

'What happened? You lose it on a pony?'

'Knicked.'

'Lifted?'

'Yeah, swiped.'

'Any kats in question?'

'Nada. All that cash for my rent. Gone.'

I was getting pissed off. Just wanted outta the house. Wasn't in the game for the guilt trip.

'Guys like that should be fuckin castrated. I mean, a girl like you, minding her own wax...'

'Done and dusted now, Charlie. Point is, no grade.'

Impulse kicked in and I said: 'Negative.'

'Don't get ya.'

'I'm good for it.'

'No way.'

'Yeah.'

'Forget it.'

'What ya gonna do?'

'Sit at home.'

'Like a Toblerone?'

'Spose so.'

'No go, tornado. Meet me in Massimo's at eight o'clock.'

She seemed to think, said: 'Hope you're flush.'

'Roger that.'

'Rendezvous at eight, then.'

We were both early. I met her at seven forty-five. Long black jumper and tight blue jeans. Her dark brown hair came down over the side of her face. She sensed me come in and looked up. Those eyes: searching, intelligent, deep. I asked: 'You wanna pint?'

'Vodka n'coke.'

'Comin up, cubes?'

'No thanks. I'm cool enough.'

Drank them. Got more. I said: 'So hit me with a life secret.'

'You first.'

'Where do I start?'

'Why you drinking Cidona?'

'I was an alcoholic at sixteen.'

'That the last time you drank?'

'Seventeen. Nine years ago.'

'You must've started young.'

'Thirteen years old. Bushes, car parks, football pitches, all scattered with flagons of cider.'

'Just cider?'

'Everything. Name the poison.'

'Interesting.'

'Who ya telling? Friend of mine was in a pub last week, in Ballinrobe, the town I'm from. He met one of the locals from the old days. Guy says: "*Where's Charlie now? I never see him.*" and my friend says: "*He don't drink no more.*" And the guy, all fulla surprise says: "*Jesus, and he was good at it too.*"'

We sipped, she asked: 'When was rock bottom?'

'Hit a cop.'

'Do any time?'

'No. Close, but too young to go down. Then

my liver nearly burst and they sent me to rehab.'

'You really weren't fuckin around...'

'One more session and I'm a dead man.'

I took a draught of Cidona. It tormented my mouth with memories of Strongbow, said: 'Your turn.'

'Travelled the last five years.'

'States?'

'No. Thailand, China, Australia, some of Europe...'

'Favourite place?'

'Prague. I'll go there again when I'm not so broke, maybe. Gettin robbed doesn't help.'

I swallowed hard, said: 'Another twist?'

'Sure, cowboy.'

Felt the first wrench of guilt. It was detrimental. Thought: what the fuck am I doin?

We stayed there till closing time. Chewing the fat, shooting the breeze, give it a name, call it talking. After, the bouncer came over, high on power, clapped and said: 'Come on, guys, love is portable.'

Drained the chalice and left.

Exterior. The Latin Quarter. Night.

I asked: 'Your place or mine?'

'Where you live?'

'Forster Court.'

'Fuck that.'

'You?'

'Moyola Park.'

'Sounds good. We get a cab?'

'Let's walk, I need the air.'

Came down by *Monroe's* and walked through the canal behind *The Roisín Dubh.* Went by the old playground, with the graffiti on the wall. This is where she saw the swings. 'I wanna swing.'

'Eh?'

'Swings. Come on.'

'Forget about it.'

'Hey! If you're comin home with me, you're goin to swing first.'

Shrugged. Thought: *What're ya gonna do?*

She hopped on and I pushed her forward. She floated back, legs out, real aerodynamic. 'I love the playground. It reminds me of being a kid.'

The conflict was starting to bite. Robbed her today, going home with her tonight. Tried to put it out of my mind. Business and pleasure. Then, fuck it. Why not? I was sending her the wallet back and gave her the dollars in vodka. Odds and evens. It's all good.

She stood up, felt dizzy, saw a bench and lay across it. Got all snug and sexy. Then, looking at the sky, she said: 'Come lie with me.'

I went over. She put her head on my knees, said: 'This is a good night.'

'Sure is.' I lit a cigarette, blew some crystals, said: 'I stole your wallet today.'

'I know.'

'What's with the catatonia?'

'I knew you'd call. This way I get free booze *and* my money back.'

Finished the smoke and walked to her place. Went through the college. Loud drunks hanging around outside the church. Shoes hanging on the power lines, sign of a dealer. Walked through Ardilaun Road and came up by Moyola Park. She lived in 49, top of the hill, light in the porch.

Exterior. Front of her house. Night.

'Guess you're coming in then?'

'Guess I am.'

Made it to the stairs. Enter passion. Luscious breasts. Skin, creamy and soft. Kissed her all around. She took off my shirt and went lower. Getting into it. Got naked and went for glory. It was animal. Hard, rough and fast. Calmed down and went upstairs.

Interior. Bedroom. Night.

Large bed, purple walls and a poster of Guevara. Stereo in the corner with a rack of tunes. Clapton, Oldfield and Moby. Put on the whale, track nine, *Extreme ways*.

Got on the bed and took in the beats. She sat on top. Her hair tickled my face and her nipples rubbed hard on my chest. Locked legs and went in.

Interior. Vagina. Moist.

It was smooth and passionate. After, went for Oldfield, *Tubular Bells*. She asked: 'What do you think about death?'

'He's a bastard.'

'Seriously.'

'He's a bastard.'

'Had much experience?'

'Once or twice. You?'

'Yeah, parents. Car accident.'

'Long ago?'

'Five years.'

'That's when you hit the road?'

'Got the fuck outta dodge. How would *you* like to go?'

'Die? Thinkin like that is dangerous for a guy like me. You?'

'I don't know. I'm in a lot of trouble right now.'

'Trouble? What kind of trouble?'

'Me and my friend bought some cocaine.'

'So?'

'So now she's dead.'

'Why?'

'They killed her.'

'Because she bought coke?'

'Because she never paid them.'

'How much?'

'Ten grand. She sold it all and tried to rip them off.'

'She doesn't sound that smart.'

'They cut her throat with a garden shears. And now I'm next. And I'm terrified.'

'Who are we talkin about?'

She gave me the name. I knew it, didn't want to hear it, but now here I am. Can't unring the fuckin bell.

I said: 'Don't worry, I'll make some calls.'

'You?'

'Me. I know them.'

'What about the money?'

'They owe me a few favours.'

She thought, said: 'Guess it makes up for robbing me.'

'And your wallet's in the post.'

'How polite. I really thought there was no way out.'

'I have ya covered.'

'I haven't felt alive in so long.'

Wrapped in the smell of our juices. Clammy and warm. She asked: 'What would you do if you heard I was dead?'

'Just met ya, kid. Tough call. What d'ya you want me to say?'

'I don't know, something profound.'

I lit a smoke, dragged heavy, thought, blew a passive cloud, said: 'Think I'd go Vodka&Red Bull, and wash it down with a pint of cider. Then chew on some Tequila worms.'

'After nine years?'

'Yeah. Then do the waltz with a bottle of Jack. World needs women like you. If y'all start dyin, then I don't wanna be round neither. No point.'

She frowned, leaned on her elbow. Put a palm under her chin and bit her baby finger, said: 'You're a cold fish.'

'I just complimented you.'

'That's not what I mean. You're like...

detached.'

'People been telling me that my whole life.'

Third time was slow, intense and sensual. Saw us through until dawn. After, the birds were singing outside and the dim light came through the curtains. We were silent in the glow of peace and lingering passion. I looked into her brown eyes. She was awake, and alert, staring right at me, like she was in a trance. I blinked, just like a photograph, and fell into my last real slumber.

In the morning, she was gone. Exit El Niño. No note. No goodbye. Got up, put on my threads and went home. Hung out in Forster Court, thought she'd call. No bells.

I gave it a few days. Knocked on a few doors, called in a few favours, got her debt cleared. It was Mickey Mouse money anyway compared to what they were making. Some of the gang wanted me back, too. Cash vans, banks, credit unions, they all needed someone with skill and experience. But I told them I was out. Clean, dry, on the straight and narrow – except for the wallets. Man has to make a pound somehow. They said the big man wanted to talk, but I declined. Send my regards, but them days are gone. Just don't fuck with El Niño or there'll be consequences.

Summer kicked in and I was busy with my trade. Kept an eye out but didn't see her. Took it as a *one-night-stand* and kept busy stealing. It was productive too, and I made a lotta dough.

Convinced myself that I didn't care, she was too wild for someone trying to stay sober and I needed to stay outta the abyss. I read books, worked out, and stole for the next three weeks but sleep was getting tough, like I'd been to the goblin market; the taste of forbidden fruit fresh on my lips.

-

Her name was El Niño. Her father called her that because the night she was born there was a storm. He said it signified the way she was to live her life. They found her by the Spanish Arch. It came over the six o'clock news. A couple of locals talking about tragedy and youth and all the rest and the paramedics, with resuscitation over, closing the ambulance doors and shaking their heads before slowly driving away.

The gang had ignored me. Violated her, sent a message that they weren't going to be told what to do by anyone. And now I'd have to retaliate. I'll give it some time. They'll be expecting me, have their guard up. But I'll let get them get lazy, let them sleep, let them dream, and then I'll visit.

I see her everywhere now. Across the street, behind a delivery van, the back of her head disappearing into a shop. Her voice calls my name from a distance. I see her in my reflection, standing behind me, hovering around like a translucent spirit. All the time I hear about storms and weather phenomena. My mind picks up on everything, like a radar for pain. Tunes from Mike

Oldfield. Moby. All sending out her echoes.

The nights are cold and long and bring demons for company. The future stays dark and numb. I spend the nights on the streets, head down, kicking stones and dodging the cracks, looking for a distraction. Nothing comes. The city is awash with students and innocence. Thoughts swirl and corruption hovers around my mind, always looking for a chink. That trance like stare, the taste of her, the smell of her hair. Rage at the loss, the guilt of not doing more, revenge roaring to be let loose.

-

The room is dark tonight with the only light coming from the television. Its muted screen shows pictures of Galway. Reports of a local gang wiped out. Brutal deaths, almost like signatures. An escalation of the recent murders of two young women. Cops looking for a man in a brown coat, known to law enforcement, considered dangerous. Report if seen, but do not approach.

The table in front of me is scattered with newspapers. Reports on what they did to her, and more recent editions on how they suffered too. Beside them is filthy plates thrown on the floor, and half rolled cigarette skins. Outside, I can hear the swish of cars on the road, driving through the corridors of innocence.

Particles of dust float through the TV's spectrum. There's a party next door and I can hear muffled laughter and the strumming of an acoustic guitar. Bottles clunk together and people run up and down the stairs. It's the bottles that get me. I'm wondering what to do. I could go out and rob, but I'm too distracted and would probably get caught. And half the fuckin world is looking for me. I thought of her again, her voice "...*cute, see you this evening....*"

I took out her picture and looked at it. Still had it from the wallet that time. Something tectonic shifts in my mind. It's the image of her. The idea that's she gone. The walls around me start to crumble. Everything I do is loud. A cup falls into the sink and rattles my nerves. In the bathroom, I turn on a tap and it sounds like amplified radio static. My reflection is like a bad portrait of someone else. I don't recognise him. Some other kat from some other world, looking back at me like a stranger. Now my hands are shaking and my legs are weak, like I have some wild fever. There are goose pimples on my neck and somewhere inside I can hear a slow throbbing vibration.

Back on the couch. Turned off the telly. I try tunes but they don't work. I can't sit still. I stand up, light a smoke and look around. My jacket's hanging on the hallstand by the door and my shadow dances behind it.

Exit Charlie.

Interior. Neachtains. Night.

They say you take up where you left off. Some things about a pub are universal. Old man at the counter. Fire going in the corner. Barman drying a glass. I give the heads up and he leaves down the towel. Hands in the back pocket, all enthusiastic. I give him my order. Four vodkas, one Red Bull, all in the same pint glass with ice. He doesn't flinch, gets it, leaves it down, like a prize that's been a long time coming. I pay and get the change. Lift it and let it swirl, take in its aroma, my brain chemistry roaring to life, addiction zombies running wild. Looked around. Not many in. Fella my age in the corner, sitting on his own, pint of lager, listening to music. He looks indifferent, content, oblivious. I'm starting to feel warm. The panic subsiding. The need taking hold. I slide my fingers round the rim of the glass. It feels cold, confident, sufficiently lethal. The chair has arms designed for the elbows. I sit back and get cosy and let a rabid desire take over.

The old man in the corner raises his pint and salutes me. I take up mine, salute him back and we drink in unison, me with less patience. It goes down fast, acidic and hard, and the breeze rustles across the back of my neck as a door slams behind me forever.

Printed in Great Britain
by Amazon